Summer Change

'Choice, not chance, determines your destiny.'
-Aristotle (384-322 BC)

Summer Change

© Melissa Wray, 2023

Cover design by Carmen Dougherty.
Layout by Wombat Books.

978-1-76111-121-1

Published by Wombat Books, 2023
PO Box 302,
Chinchilla QLD 4413
Australia
www.wombatrhiza.com.au

A catalogue record for this
book is available from the
National Library of Australia

Summer Change

MELISSA WRAY

rhiza edge

For Carol, Anna and Carolyn.
Cousins are always the first best friend. Xo

Chapter 1

My parents were liars. Dirty. Big. Liars. They were hiding something from me, and I was going to find out what. But first I had to conquer this damn fence. I dragged myself halfway up, fighting the urge to jump back down.

'Ouch.' The wood bit into my fingers as they curled over the top.

'If I can do it, so can you,' my cousin, Lexi, taunted from above.

My bare toes gripped the ledge as a tremor vibrated through my calves.

'It's easy, Shae.' Lexi waved her arms about. 'Look, no hands!'

I ignored her teasing and concentrated on the climb. The first time my dad took me on a Ferris wheel was the last time I'd flirted with heights. We had just taken our seats as the carriage jerked upwards. The hum in my throat was soft at first, but it soon escalated to an ear-piercing scream. We only managed one spin before the attendant stopped the ride to let me off.

'Come on.' Lexi banged the wooden palings. 'It'll be tea-time soon.'

I hauled myself upwards, twisted awkwardly, then plopped on the corner of the intersecting fences. 'I was trying not to get a splinter.'

'You're such a baby, Shae. I can't believe you're still afraid of heights.'

I poked my tongue out and tried to stay balanced. I had no

plans to go splat on the ground below.

Lexi laughed. 'So, *cuz*, what did you do to get stuck with us all summer?'

'Why, what did you hear?'

She shook her head. 'Nothing. It was a joke.'

I sighed. 'Then you know as much as me.'

Lexi swept her hair around her neck so it flowed down the front of one shoulder. She tucked the silken strands behind her ear. Each one sat perfectly in place, just like in a shampoo commercial. Meanwhile, the shadow of my curly mop spread across my legs. Most days I didn't even bother to try and control the frizz.

'Shae, is something going on with you and your parents?' asked Lexi.

'Like what?'

'I don't know. It's just … things were tense when they dropped you off. Plus, your visit happened kind of suddenly.'

'It won't be for the whole summer, and you'll get to have fun with Lexi,' said Mum.

'I have no idea what happened. Dad's hardly spoken to me lately and Mum's been weird. Even more than normal.' I rolled my eyes.

'I thought you were all going to New Zealand?' said Lexi.

'We were! The 'trip of a lifetime' before I started year twelve. Dad even said he'd go white water rafting with me.' I shrugged. 'One minute we were excited about it then, bam! No more trip of a lifetime.'

'We need to cancel, Shae. There's something your father and I have to deal with.'

They both didn't look at each other when they shattered our holiday plans. Dad couldn't even make eye contact with me. As though it were somehow my fault the trip had to be cancelled.

'But something must have happened,' Lexi persisted. 'People don't just change their mind about overseas holidays like that.'

I shrugged. 'Mum gave some stupid excuse and blamed work, but I know she's lying.'

'*Keep your voice down, Shae's home. We can discuss it later.*' Mum's harsh words last week confirmed my suspicions. Something was going on that they didn't want me to know about. It was so typical of Mum not to involve me. She still treated me like a kid learning to tie shoelaces, not someone who just got their license.

Lexi nudged me. 'I love that we can hang out, but I'm here if you want to talk.'

'Thanks, Lexi.'

My cousin was flaky at times, but she would jump in front of a moving bus for those she loved. We were born two weeks apart and she loved to remind me that I'm the baby of the family.

'Let's forget all that secret stuff, Shayzie. We're going to have the best summer ever!' Lexi grabbed my hand and jiggled it about.

My body shook and came dangerously close to wobbling right off the ledge. 'Lexi, be *careful*!' Breathe in. Breathe out. Deep breath in. Deep breath out. I worked to calm my nerves.

The smell of barbeque sausages wafted past and distracted me. My stomach grumbled, reminding me that I hadn't eaten breakfast. I searched the neighbours' backyards to find the source of the teasing aroma. In the yard behind us a golden Labrador lazed outside the kennel, ignoring the chewed tennis balls strewn across the grass. On the right side was an aged weatherboard house. Specks of dirty, white paint had flaked off the wood. The fly wire screens hung at odd angles and the grass was overgrown and littered with yellow daisies. It had the opposite look to our modern home. Mum planned the style while Dad chose the gadgets. It took months of trailing around display homes looking at the same, boring things.

'Hey, does that old guy still sing those songs?' I asked.

Lexi followed my gaze. 'Mr. Sampson? Yeah, sometimes we can

hear him. It still sounds more like groaning than singing.'

'Remember the first time we heard him?'

He had been sitting in the wooden rocking chair near his back door. We were worried he was going to have a heart attack from the noises he was making.

'Trust me, his singing hasn't got any better.' said Lexi.

Mr. Sampson was quiet compared to the previous people. There were four kids in that family, the same as Lexi's. But compared to my cousins Dale, Aileen, Blake and Lexi, the others were twice as loud and never silent when they were home.

I watched the house for any signs of life. The lace curtain shifted in the kitchen window, but nobody appeared.

Lexi poked me. 'Are you going to jump sometime today?'

I snapped back to attention and focused on the pool below. It reminded me of a giant bowl of jelly with hidden delights. We had jumped into it many times over the years. I hated the height, but it was worth the adrenaline rush.

'I can do this,' I muttered to myself as I stood reluctantly and adjusted my new bikini. It was a guilt gift from Mum to make up for the cancelled trip. She'd screwed up her face at the buttercup colour. *'It looks like melted cheese.'* I made her buy it anyway, but now I kind of wish I'd listened to her fashion advice. I would never admit that to her though.

'Come on, Shayzie. You can do it!'

I leant on Lexi's shoulder to steady myself. With arms stretched out in front, I took a deep breath and jumped. Nothing but air and space surrounded me. I tried not to think about the impact to come. Instead, I curled into a ball and completed a full somersault. *Splash!* I broke through the cool surface then pushed off the bottom of the pool.

I burst through the water grinning. 'Did you see that? I did it!'

There was no response. I wiped the water from my face and looked above. Lexi was no longer perched on the fence. I looked around the manicured backyard, but there was no sign of her.

'Lexi?' I reached for my necklace and gripped the blue agate stone. A gift from Dad on my sixteenth birthday: meant to emanate strength.

'*Lexi?*' My voice echoed back through the silence as I clambered out of the pool. 'Lexi, where are you?'

Suddenly a groan drifted across from Mr. Sampson's side of the fence.

'*Lexi!*' I ran toward the noise and scrambled up the fence. The ground swirled up to meet me and I squeezed my eyes shut. Once the vertigo passed, I opened them again.

'Ooww.' A low, moaning growl sounded from below.

I peered over the fence and stifled a laugh. Lexi lay flat on her back, arms and legs bent like an upside-down turtle wearing a bikini.

'I'm ... win ... winded,' she said.

I ignored my racing heart, swung my legs over the fence and jumped down to help her. I moved cautiously toward my cousin. There was no blood spurting anywhere and her limbs pointed in all the right directions.

'Don't just ... stare at ... me. Help ... me up.'

I carefully pulled her to her feet. She wrapped her arms around her middle and doubled over. Her face grimaced as she tried to catch her breath.

'Are you hurt?' I asked.

Leaves and twigs stuck to her blonde hair. It looked like the finch's nest in our backyard. I tried to brush the dirt and grass off, but Lexi swatted my hand away. She took deeper breaths until her breathing returned to normal. Slowly, she stood up and clasped her hands to her chest.

'What happened?' I tried to keep a straight face, but it was hard with the vision of her turtle pose still fresh in my mind.

'I lost my balance because *you* pushed too hard when you jumped. You could have killed me.' She shoved past me.

There was a small graze on her elbow and a bruise had started to darken around it. Otherwise, she was still in a perfect, flawless condition.

'Don't be such a drama queen. You wouldn't die from that height.' I smirked, but Lexi was not amused.

'I just *fell* off the *fence*! A bit of concern please.' She flicked her long blonde hair over her shoulders and climbed upwards. I started to follow, but something caught my interest.

'What are you doing? Let's go.' Lexi disappeared over the fence.

A gold linked bracelet lay nestled in the long blades of grass. I crouched down for a closer look.

It was engraved on the smooth, rectangular space. *Sondra.* I scrunched it up before Lexi saw. The bracelet must be somebody's, but there was only Mr. Sampson next door. It might have been from the previous family, except there was nobody called Sondra. *Who else could it belong to?* I stared at the crumbling house and the curtain settled again. A shiver trickled down my spine. I climbed over the dividing fence without looking back.

Chapter 2

'Tea's ready,' my older cousin, Blake, yelled from the back porch.

I followed Lexi as she slid open the back door and entered the kitchen. A garlic smell instantly made my mouth water. Aunty Liz stirred the Bolognese sauce on the stove.

'Hope you're hungry, Shae,' she said.

'I'm starving and pasta's my favourite.'

'Do you remember when we told Lexi that spaghetti could come out her mouth *and* nose at the same time?' said Blake.

I laughed. 'She shoved the pasta up there to see if it was true.'

'I had to take her to the doctor's two weeks later because there was still pasta in there,' Aunty Liz said. 'It was starting to sprout!'

'Give me a break, I was six,' said Lexi. 'How was I meant to know?'

'Hello, family!' A deep voice called out. Uncle Kevin's footsteps clumped down the hallway and entered the kitchen.

'Hi, kids.' Uncle Kevin took off Blake's hat and tossed it on the table, then he removed Lexi's sunglasses. He stepped behind my aunt and kissed her cheek. 'Evening my love.' He towered over her small frame.

'Eww!' said Lexi. 'Children present.'

Uncle Kevin snorted. 'Children? I thought we were all grown-ups in this house. At least that's what you keep trying to tell me.'

Lexi rolled her eyes and shoved the blue glasses back on her head. Sunglasses were her weakness. She had a different colour and style to match all her outfits.

Aunty Liz moved out of my uncle's clutches toward the sink and poured the pasta into a colander. The steam fogged up her glasses.

Uncle Kevin turned to me. 'Hi, Shae, how was your first day here?'

'We swam in the pool,' Lexi answered for me.

'Lexi spent most of the day on her back.' I raised an eyebrow. Taunting her, threatening to share her embarrassment from the fall today. Lexi shook her head from side to side. Her scowl crept upwards and I knew I was forgiven for her near-death experience.

'What *did* you two do today?' asked Blake.

The story was too funny not to share with him, but I remained quiet for Lexi's sake. Besides, we have been told a hundred times not to climb the fence and jump into the pool. Especially after the time Blake landed on my oldest cousin, Dale, and gave him a concussion.

'Lexi, put the cutlery out please,' said Aunty Liz.

'Can I help?' I asked.

'Did you kids hear that? Help being offered! It's a miracle,' she teased my cousins.

'Hey, we all know I'm more help than Lexi is,' said Blake, shoving his sister out of the way.

'Cut it out,' said Lexi, shoving him back.

They continued to push each other around the kitchen table. Lexi was younger than Blake by less than a year. Aunty Liz always joked she needed to even up the family fast so Aileen wasn't outnumbered in the middle of two brothers. When Lexi and Blake were kids, they liked to tell people they were twins.

'Shae, you can get drinks,' Aunty Liz said, pouring the drained pasta into a ceramic bowl.

I removed the glasses and poured water for everyone. Blake put the bowl of Bolognese sauce in the middle of the table as Aunty Liz placed the pasta beside it.

'Let's eat!' She clapped her hands.

I loaded the pasta onto my plate and added some tossed green salad. Lexi passed the garlic bread and I swiped two pieces before passing it along.

'Have you spoken to your mum yet, Shae?' asked Uncle Kevin, scratching his beard.

'Oops, the cheese.' Aunty Liz jumped up to get it. She squeezed Uncle Kevin's shoulder and shook her head.

'Err, not yet, but Mum said she'd probably call tonight.'

Uncle Kevin nodded. 'Your mum has a lot going on at the moment.'

I looked up, sharply. *What was that supposed to mean?*

Aunty Liz dropped the parmesan cheese on the table. 'I'm sure Susannah will call when she has time, Kevin.' She smiled, but the skin around her eyes didn't crinkle.

'What about your dad?' Uncle Kevin said. 'Have you heard from him?'

Aunty Liz took a deep breath but stayed focused on the spaghetti.

'Nope, not yet.' *What's with the sudden interest in my parents?*

'They're probably having too much fun without you.' Blake wiggled his eyebrows, but nobody laughed.

Everyone knew how cocooned my world was. I got my first mobile phone when I was ten because Mum was such a control freak. My friends thought I was so lucky to have one, but it didn't even have the internet! Calls and text messages only.

It was strange that I hadn't heard from either of them, not even a text message. Even when Dad travelled for work, he always called me. I spun my fork around until there was a wad of spaghetti. I

9

shoved it into my mouth, trying to ignore the questions forming.

'Guess who I ran into today? Nadine that used to live next door,' said Aunty Liz, closing the topic of my parents.

'Hope her zits have cleared up,' said Lexi.

'Be nice,' said Blake. 'Nadine's cute.'

'What were the other sisters called?' I asked.

'Bethany, Clara and Naomi, why?' said Lexi.

'No reason, I just forgot.' They didn't match *Sondra* from the mystery bracelet.

I reached for my agate stone, only to find nothing there. 'Oh no, my necklace! I was wearing it when we were swimming earlier. What if the pool filters have sucked it up?'

'We can look for it after tea. It'll turn up,' said Uncle Kevin.

I forced a smile and tapped at the empty space on my throat.

'So, what did Nadine have to say?' asked Blake. 'Did she ask about me?'

'She didn't ask about you, my darling, but she did just start a hairdressing apprenticeship.'

Lexi snorted. 'That figures. She probably still sleeps on a satin pillowcase so her hair doesn't tangle. She wouldn't even go in the pool in case the chlorine dried out her *luscious locks*.'

'She wasn't that bad,' said Blake.

'That's because you were too busy spying on her through the fence,' said Lexi.

'I never spied. She knew I watched her.'

'Eww. You're such a pervert.' Lexi threw a crust at him.

'Hey! You're sweeping that up,' said Aunty Liz. 'Oh, Nadine gave me something for you, Lexi.' Aunty Liz retrieved a pamphlet. *Summer Special. Blonde Highlights. $60.*

'That bitch.'

'*Lexi!*'

'What? As if I need highlights.' Lexi fluffed her golden hair. 'The sun lightens my hair naturally.'

'Oh yeah?' said Blake. 'What about when you sprayed it red?'

'Shut up! It was copper.'

'Your mother had the blondest hair in summer, Shae.' said Aunty Liz. 'It was almost white when she was a little girl. Our mum, that is your Nanna, called it fairy floss hair because it was so thin but still sat perfectly.'

'I wish I'd got the blonde hair in the family,' I said. 'Instead of this ... whatever it is.'

'Your hair is a beautiful auburn shade,' said Aunty Liz, reaching across to touch it. 'You should embrace it. And people pay good money for those curls.'

I pulled on the frizz that gave me nothing but grief. The best I could do was pull it back and hope it didn't spring out. Suddenly the house phone rang and everyone looked at me.

'Ten bucks that's your folks,' said Blake.

Aunty Liz jumped up and answered it. Her eyes flitted to me. 'We're not interested.' She hung up. 'Silly telemarketers. They always ring at tea-time.'

'You better pay up that ten bucks,' I said to Blake, trying to hide my disappointment.

Chapter 3

The next day Lexi and I walked from her house in Kirwan, along the track and across the Black Weir bridge. We continued until we could see the dog park across the river. I perched beside the river bank. The surface from the flat rock warmed my legs. The Ross River was nearly fifty kilometres of waterway that wound through Townsville, providing the water supply. The flow was controlled by the dam and passed through the Gleeson Weir that stretched out before me. During the rainy season the water roared over the edge creating a waterfall. When we were younger, Uncle Kevin would bring us to watch it. There wasn't even a trickle today, just the dry, scorching heat closing in.

I gazed at the cement ledge where Lexi stood in the middle. It ran across the river dividing this level from the one below. The drop was only a couple of meters, but one slip and you could be in serious trouble. If the water was higher, it would be lapping at her ankles.

'Come on, Shae, it's great out here,' Lexi called out. 'The view is beautiful!'

The platform looked easy to cross, but I was not fooled. It was a danger zone. I'd seen it become a raging torrent without much warning. After heavy rain it flowed fast and furious and you didn't want to be caught where Lexi stood, or you might be swept to a watery death.

A branch snapped beside me and a familiar looking person appeared.

'Mikayla!' I jumped up and hugged her.

Lexi and Mikayla had been friends for years. The three of us often hung out when I came to stay. Mikayla waved to Lexi who made her way back toward us.

'I love your hair,' I said. 'It's very rock chick, but in a cute, softer way!'

Mikayla ran her fingers through the pixie crop. 'I'm still getting used to it. Mum flipped out when I cut it all off. You don't think the purple is too much?'

'Are you questioning your fashion sense?' I asked.

'No! But it might be a bit extreme, even for me.'

I reached across to touch it. 'It suits you. I love it!'

Mikayla seemed different, older. It wasn't just the edgy haircut. Her cut off denim shorts were so short the pockets hung out the bottom. Blue mascara thickened her lashes and black liner framed her eyes. My face was free of make-up with fluffy hair tamed by a bandana tied in a knot. Some flyaway strands of hair tickled my nose and I quickly pushed them behind my ears, suddenly self-conscious of my bland style.

'You're still not tempted to cross?' Mikayla gestured toward the Weir.

'Ahh, no thanks. I value my life too much.'

'Go on! There hasn't been a croc sighting for at least a month,' Mikayla teased.

The urban myth of crocodiles lurking in the Weir had floated around for years. There had been many stories, including some grainy images shared as proof. Everybody knew somebody who had, once upon a time, seen a croc in the river. Even Uncle Kevin told us how he and his mates thought they saw one when they were kids.

Lexi finally reached the two of us. 'Mikayla, you made it. Yay!' She hugged her friend with a kiss on the cheek.

'I nearly didn't get here when Mum started going on about getting a job this summer and my messy room. Urggh, she drives me crazy.' Mikayla pulled out a cigarette from the front pocket of her backpack. 'At least I managed to pinch this from her.'

I smiled, uncertain what else to do. This was a new habit since my last visit. Mikayla lit one end of the stick and dragged on the other. Her lips puckered up as she blew the plume of smoke out. She offered it to me, but I shook my head.

'Don't tell Blake, okay?' Lexi said, reaching for the cigarette.

I screwed up my nose. 'Since when do you smoke?'

'Don't be so judgy, cuz.' Lexi sucked on the end of the stick.

'I'm not judging, I'm just … surprised,' I said. 'Don't you need to be fit to dance?'

Lexi passed the cigarette back. 'I dance fine with or without smoking,' she snapped.

Lexi had been swirling and twirling since she was small. Her room was decorated with all kinds of medals and ribbons she'd won over the years. She always trained hard to be fit, at least she used to. Maybe that wasn't her thing anymore.

'Are the others still coming?' Mikayla asked.

Lexi sat down, away from me. 'They should be here any minute.'

I didn't even know Mikayla was meeting us. What else had Lexi organised?

As if on cue, voices drifted through the trees. Leaves crunched as three guys appeared in the clearing. They strode toward us, each dressed in a singlet and board shorts. They looked like Babushka dolls in order from tallest to smallest. Lexi and Mikayla jumped up to greet them. The taller guy moved toward Lexi. He drew her in and his thick arms circled her slim frame.

'I'm glad you called,' he growled into her neck.

She giggled as he kissed her cheek. She melted even further into him then winked at me. A minute ago, she wouldn't even look at me. Now she was showing off her latest crush. Talk about a mood swing.

'This is my boyfriend, Kai.' She wrapped her arm around him. 'This is my cousin, Shae. The one I told you about.'

My eyes narrowed at her tone. Lexi pushed her sunglasses on top of her head, waiting for my reaction. Was I meant to be impressed because she had a boyfriend? Or because it was this guy?

Kai nodded but barely looked at me. It was obvious why he came to the Weir today, and it sure wasn't to meet me. Lexi introduced the other two guys, Simon and Brendan. Mikayla moved closer to the one called Brendan. That just left Simon who waved at me, then looked around as though he'd rather be anywhere but here.

Kai grabbed Lexi's hand and pulled her out toward the Weir. 'Let's cross it.'

She giggled and resisted. 'It's really high! What if I fall?'

He pulled her in close. 'I won't let you fall.' Lexi shoved him away and ran onto the Weir, all signs of fear gone as her long legs skipped across the concrete ledge.

I shook my head at her games. Kai didn't look like much of a player. Lexi pointed her finger at him, then curled it inwards. He marched toward her, as though on a mission to catch his prey. I turned around toward the others, only to find Mikayla had deserted me as well!

She had moved inside the cement cave with Brendan. Over time the steps had weathered into the wall, making it easy to climb into. The space was deep, as though someone had dug it out. Mikayla and Brendan were already entwined in a lock-jaw embrace with each other. *Could this get any worse?* My skin prickled and I desperately wanted to get out of here. I looked away quickly, before they caught me spying on them.

Simon stood near me. With hands shoved in his pockets, he rocked on his feet. He blew a bubble before his gum popped. Great, now what was I going to do? Mikayla was in the love cave. Kai had coaxed Lexi across the water. Meanwhile, I was left alone with this stranger. Some guy I had just met but had already been paired off with. Was Simon meant to babysit me? Lexi had probably set up this whole thing just so she could be with Kai. Alone. Then she wouldn't have to feel guilty about leaving me by myself. What was up with her this visit? She never would have done this any other time. Lexi and I had always been close, ever since we were little girls. I loved staying with her and the rest of the family. But something about her was seriously different this trip.

Another idea made me cringe. I couldn't believe I didn't think of it as soon as the guys arrived. Three guys. Three girls. Duh! Maybe Lexi hoped I would hook up with Simon? Or maybe her new boyfriend talked her into setting this up. No way! Lexi knew me better than that. Besides, I didn't need my cousin setting me up with some random guy I'd never see again. Simon smiled at me and I took a step back. Lexi might know better, but this guy didn't.

Chapter 4

'Kai said you're not from around here,' said Simon, breaking the awkward silence.

'Have you guys been talking about me?'

Simon shrugged. 'He just said you're Lexi's cousin, and you're from out of town.'

I could imagine how that conversation *really* went. 'I'm visiting from Airlie Beach,' I said.

'Nice place.' He blew a bubble. 'How long are you staying in Townsville?'

'Good question,' I muttered.

When the trip to New Zealand got cancelled my parents said I had to stay here. But they never said for how long.

'If you're supposed to be hanging out with Lexi that might be hard. I think she could be gone for a while,' he said, eyebrows raised in a knowing way.

I looked across the Weir. The edge was bordered with bushes, but Lexi was nowhere to be seen. She wouldn't do anything in broad daylight, would she? That would be trashy and not the Lexi I knew. I was certain she'd never gone all the way, but then again what would I know? I only just discovered her smoking habit. Maybe she had started doing other new things as well.

'So, what are *we* going to do?' Simon asked.

'What do you think we're going to do?' I retreated further away from him.

'Nothing! I was kidding, geez.' He raised his hands in surrender. 'You looked at me like I was a murderer.'

'Maybe not a murderer,' I crossed my arms. 'But definitely sketchy.' I reached for my necklace out of habit, then remembered it was still missing.

Simon scooped up a couple of pebbles. He moved downstream from the lovers behind us. They were still linking tongues in the love cave. Simon skimmed a stone across the water's surface. It bounced a couple of times before it sank. He threw one to me, but I fumbled the catch.

'Butter-fingers, hey?'

I snatched the pebble from the ground and joined him. 'I'm actually very coordinated.'

That wasn't true. In fact, the only thing I could keep balanced on was my bike. Simon skimmed another stone across the water. Ripples vibrated out from the point of impact. I tried to copy Simon's action. I took aim, released and failed. *Plop.*

'You have to flick your wrist a bit more. Try and make the stone bounce across the top.' He flicked his wrist to demonstrate and the stone skimmed several times before sinking.

I grabbed another pebble and took aim. This time it managed to bounce twice.

'You're getting better already,' he said.

I threw a stone at him. 'I don't need your pity praise.'

Simon laughed. The sound helped me relax a bit.

He picked up another stone. 'Here, try this one.'

I rubbed it between my hands, as if that might help. I took

aim, swung my arm back, then paused. Movement on the other side of the Weir distracted me just as Lexi burst from the bushes. She stopped, turned back and gestured wildly before stomping toward the crossing. Kai ran after her. She ignored him and continued across the narrow ledge. Kai tried to get her attention but she knocked his arm away. She lost her balance in the process and teetered on the edge. Kai pulled her back, but the effort caused him to lose balance and he disappeared from view. Lexi reached out toward him, then slipped over the edge herself.

'*Kai.*' Simon ran toward the water.

'*Lexi.*' I ran down to the concrete crossing.

I started to cross but the watery depths below blurred together and made me sway. I crouched down to steady myself. What was I thinking? I couldn't walk out along the ledge. The drop was steep and the bottom murky. I'd never been out that far before.

'*Help,*' screamed Lexi.

My head snapped up. Lexi had managed to get herself balanced half on the ledge and half with legs dangling. She couldn't hang on much longer. With a deep breath, I moved toward her. Her hands were my focus as I tried not to think about how high up from the water we were. Climbing the back fence yesterday was nothing compared to this fresh hell. I wanted to crouch down again and crawl, but that would take too long. With one foot in front of the other I finally reached her. Kneeling on the concrete, I leaned backward to try and lever her up. Lexi hooked her knee on the ledge, then slowly hoisted herself upwards.

Once she was safe, I searched the river for Kai. An oversized shadow lurked below the water and I shuddered. Then I saw Kai sitting on the riverbank, sopping wet.

'He's safe,' I said, flopping onto the ledge.

Lexi looked up at me. A grin crept upwards, then she started to laugh.

'Why are you laughing?' I asked.

'You! You're on the Weir.'

It was then I realised how far out I was. My hands shook and I tried to squash the fear. 'I don't see how this is funny.'

'If I'd known this would get you to cross, I would have *pretended* to fall ages ago.'

'Pretended?' She couldn't have been faking. The fear on her face was clear. Or maybe she was a better actress than I gave her credit for. 'What are you talking about, Lexi?'

'You should have seen your face!' Lexi snorted.

My stomach dropped. 'What the hell do you mean, *pretended*?'

Kai stood from the bank and gave me a thumbs up. That's when I noticed he was no longer wearing his sneakers or t-shirt. This deception had been planned all along. Lexi blew him a kiss then gave me a gentle shove.

'Looks like you can cross the Weir after all, Shayzie.'

'You … tricked me?'

'I wish we got it on video, but I knew you could do it. You just needed some motivation!'

Lexi skipped over the crossing toward a smug Kai. They both waved before returning to the secluded bushes.

My cousin's little stunt sank in. What had she promised Kai for him to go along with her idea? That wasn't a joke. It was a cruel prank. Was this revenge for her falling off the fence? Or because of the smoking comment?

Simon appeared beside me, but I couldn't look at him.

'Did you know they were going to do that?' I asked.

'Do what?'

Tears stung my eyes. 'Kai didn't fall. They *tricked* me just to get me out here. Lexi knows I don't cross the Weir wall. She knows I'm afraid of heights.'

'That's a shitty thing to do.' His gum popped loud like a snapping branch.

'Yeah, it is. Then she went and left me here. Alone. What kind of person does that?'

Your parents. I squashed the voice. I didn't want to think about them leaving me alone with my cousins for the summer.

'You're not alone.' Simon sat down beside me. 'I'm here, and it's your lucky day because I've got nowhere better to be.'

I knew he was trying to be nice about the stunt that Lexi and Kai had just pulled, but I couldn't laugh or even smile. My entire body was wound tight and ready to snap. Lexi had never done anything so mean before. My heart pounded, but I kept looking at the treetops, determined not to give in to the fear. Breathe in. Breathe out. Deep breath in. Deep breath out. After a while I followed his gaze across the horizon.

'You ever been to South Australia?' Simon asked. 'My dad is in the army and he was stationed there for two years. Do you know there's at least fifteen degrees difference between their winter and ours? Brrr.'

He was trying to take my mind off what just happened, and it was working. As Simon smiled a dent appeared in his chin. I was tempted to push my thumb against it.

'Have you moved around much?' I asked.

He nodded. 'Army families are like migrating animals. We're always on the move.'

'Does it bother you, all the moving?'

'Sometimes, but you get used to it. Plus, it can be fun checking out new places.'

I shook my head. 'I can't imagine moving all the time. I've lived in two houses my whole life and only ever in Airlie Beach.'

'Moving's not that bad. I get to meet nice people, like you …' His voice drifted off.

The tension in my body began to release as I took in the view before us. Paperbark trees lined the edge of the river. The green leaves cast a scattering of shadows against the brown water, creating a camouflage of colour. It was so still and clear that it reminded me of an oil painting I'd once seen hanging in an art gallery.

Lexi was right, it was beautiful from out here. But I was not admitting that to her. In fact, she would be lucky if I ever spoke to her again.

Chapter 5

'We'll be together again.

   Just give me some more time baby.'

The radio played loudly in the background. It was a rock song I'd never heard before. I spooned a heaped teaspoon of chocolate powder into the milk. It became a thick sludge as I stirred it around. I licked the spoon and the grit stuck to my tongue. *Clang!* The metal landed in the sink, loud and angry. I still hadn't heard from Mum or Dad, which added to my bad mood today. Lexi was watching me, but I continued to ignore her.

'I would have pretended to fall ages ago.'

She apologised again after we got home from the Weir, but I had hardly said anything to her since. If she wanted to show off in front of Kai that was fine, but she better keep me out of it from now on. He didn't seem worth the effort anyway.

'Are you two having a lover's tiff?' said Blake as he rummaged through the fridge.

'We're fine,' we said in unison.

I glugged the milk down, but it was bland and unsatisfying.

'Guess what? I heard from Mikayla that the guy next door was in jail!' Lexi said.

'Mr. Sampson's a criminal?' said Blake. 'What did he do, hold up the lawn bowls club?'

'Not him you idiot.' Lexi slapped his hat off his head. 'The guy staying there.'

'What do you mean he's been in jail? And how would Mikayla even know that?' Blake asked, stuffing toast into his mouth.

'Well not jail exactly. More like juvenile detention or something. Anyway, Mikayla said, that Brendan told her, he was thrown out of his last school for beating some guy to death.'

I snorted.

'Well, maybe not to death,' said Lexi. 'But so bad that the guy spent months in hospital.'

'What's his name?' said Blake.

Blake played for the local rugby club. He prided himself on knowing everyone around the place.

Lexi shrugged. 'I don't know who the guy was that got bashed, but the guy staying next door is Kieran, or something like that. I asked Kai, but he wouldn't talk about it. I think he knew the guy who was put in hospital.'

Blake beat his chest. 'Well, the thug better not cause any trouble around here. I'll make sure of it.'

Lexi threw a tea-towel at him. He caught it and twirled it up, ready to flick her. She squealed and ran to hide behind me.

'Get away from me. I'm not helping you,' I said.

Blake gave up without even trying to flick her. He leaned across the sink to look out the kitchen window. 'I haven't seen anyone new next door, have either of you?'

'I did! Mr. Sampson told Mum his grandson was staying, so it must be the guy.' Lexi poked me. 'Have *you* seen him? Ho-ttie!'

I rinsed out the glass and continued to ignore her, not interested in any gossip about some new guy who may or may not have a criminal record. Lexi's face drooped at my lack of enthusiasm.

'Not everyone drools over guys like you, Lexi,' said Blake.

'He must have a rockin' bod underneath those clothes,' she continued, undeterred. 'You know when you can just tell from the way their t-shirt clings.'

Lexi was always boy crazy, even when we were younger. 'Well, I haven't seen the new attraction yet,' I said.

'Make sure you keep your eyes peeled for tall, dark and handsome.'

Lexi wasn't going to let it go, and that was one of the things I loved about her. She had an enthusiasm that was infectious. I felt myself start to thaw toward her. It was hard to stay mad at Lexi for long.

'Hey, I think that's him!' Lexi pointed out the kitchen window.

I looked out to see shaggy brown hair covering a familiar face. The owner of it reached into his car and retrieved a bag. He slammed the door shut and looked at me. There was no mistaking that glare. My heart plummeted. If that guy was staying next door, we might have a problem.

I remembered my first day here. I was still mad at my parents so I went for an early morning bike ride and was nearly home. I didn't even see the car reversing from Mr. Sampson's driveway, but the driver mustn't have looked either. Neither of us stopped until it was almost too late and I thumped his boot. The brake lights flicked on and the driver got out.

'Don't you look?' he said.

I jumped off my bike. 'Ever heard of a rear-view mirror?'

'You cyclists think you own the road.'

'Well bad drivers like you should be more careful,' I said.

We both stared at each other. I wasn't backing down.

'No worries, Princess.' He slouched back in his car and slammed the door.

'Idiot,' I muttered.

He revved the car, the wheels screeched and he took off along the street. I hadn't seen him again, until now.

'Well, what do you think?' Lexi asked.

I shrugged and moved away from the window. 'He's okay.'

'Okay? Do you need your eyes checked? He's cute.'

I swatted her hand away from my face. 'I said he was okay. What more do you want?'

She huffed. 'He's probably not your type anyway.'

'What does *that* mean?' My voice rose.

'Nothing. I just meant you're probably used to hanging out with a certain type of guy. You know, the private school variety. Not the rough and just out of jail kind.'

'Are you calling me a snob?' I asked.

'No, I just meant you move in different circles to him. It makes sense you wouldn't be interested. Why so touchy today?'

It seemed the prank yesterday wasn't enough to hurt and embarrass me, now she had to insult me as well.

'Just ignore her,' Blake said. 'Lexi spoke without thinking. She does that a lot.'

I shoved a water bottle into my backpack and hooked it over my shoulders. 'I'm going for a ride.'

Neither cousin tried to stop me, nor did they offer to join me like they often did. I stomped down the hallway, but could still hear their conversation about me.

'Go easy on her, Lexi, geez,' said Blake, sticking up for me.

'It's not my fault the truth hurts her feelings,' said Lexi.

'Lexi! What's the matter with you? She's your cousin which makes her family, so calm down and give her a break while she's staying here.'

I kept walking and ignored their comments. So, Lexi thought I was a snob and Blake thought I was precious. That was just perfect.

26

I passed the glass bowl on the stand and an envelope caught my attention. My name had been scrawled across the front.

'That's weird.' I shoved it inside my backpack to deal with later.

The front door slammed behind me as I walked toward the garage. I could feel Lexi watching me from the kitchen window. I looked up and held her gaze until she moved out of view. I dragged my bike out and pushed against the tyres to check the air pressure.

'Morning, Princess.' The guy from next door leant casually against the porch, hair flopped over one eye. 'Going to pick a fight with some more cars?' he asked.

His smug face taunted me across the yard. I reached down and grabbed a yellow tennis ball lying in the doorway.

'Why don't you go get some driving lessons?' I said. My throw was wild, but the tennis ball managed to hit the wooden pole beside him, narrowly missing his head.

He stared at me, a hint of amusement on his face. He crossed his arms, as though waiting for my next move. Instead, I straddled my bike, clipped the helmet on and rode down the driveway without a backward glance. I felt his gaze boring into me. I cringed and waited for the tennis ball to connect with my back, but it didn't. As I continued along the street, I allowed myself a small victory smile.

Chapter 6

Mr. Sampson's porch was empty when I returned. Part of me expected a tennis ball to come flying out of nowhere. His car was there so he couldn't be far away. I didn't need another run in with that hot-head from next door.

My legs ached as I stretched the tension out. Things always felt better after a ride. I parked my bike before noticing how quiet it was. Blake's car was gone, but Lexi should still be here. Her music usually blared through the house, but today it was silent inside. Maybe Kai picked her up so she could ditch me again.

I followed the path down the side of the house. The gate squeaked open and there was Lexi baking on the sun-lounger beside the pool. Her bright red sunglasses covered half her face. I immediately felt guilty for the thoughts of being ditched. This fighting between us was stupid. We needed to clear the air. I'd only been here a few days and we'd already snapped at each other twice. It had never been this difficult before. What had changed?

I made my way across the yard. Her earphones throbbed with music and she was oblivious to my approach. I moved closer until a shadow fell across her face. Lexi looked up and tried to hide the surprise. She slowly removed the ear pieces, as though stalling for time to decide what to say.

'I'm sorry …' we began at the same time.

'Me first.' I pulled the other sun-lounger across and sat down. 'I shouldn't have snapped before. I was still annoyed about the dumb prank you pulled yesterday and lost it. I'm sorry.'

'I really am sorry about the whole Weir thing. I didn't think it would upset you so much,' Lexi said. 'And I honestly didn't mean anything by that stupid comment earlier. I don't think you're a snob.'

I shrugged. 'Maybe I am a bit of a snob, but without meaning to be. We both know I'm kept pretty sheltered from things.'

Lexi sat her sunglasses on top of her head. 'You are protected by your parents but who cares? Doesn't make it a bad thing.'

I laughed because it was true. My parents kept a pretty tight rein on what I could and couldn't do. That's why I loved coming to stay in Townsville with my cousins. Freedom was always available in this house. My aunty and uncle had rules, but they were reasonable.

Lexi sat up straight and grabbed my hands. 'Shae, you're my favourite cousin.'

'I'm your only cousin,' I reminded her.

'That's true, but you're still the best. I don't want us to fight,' she said.

I held up my ring finger. Lexi gripped it with hers as we shook them about.

'Do you remember when we first started using this secret shake? I had the biggest crush on Julian from school and swore you to secrecy!' said Lexi.

I laughed. 'What about when I stole five bucks from Mum's purse? I felt so guilty that I snuck it back without spending a cent, and made you promise never to tell anyone.'

We laughed again, letting go of each other's finger. I hoped this was a good time to bring up something else that had been bothering me.

'Lexi, you know when you asked if there was something going

on with my parents?'

She nodded.

'Well, it works both ways. Is there anything going on that you want to talk about?' I asked.

She looked down, unable to hold my gaze.

'You just seem different these holidays to how you normally are,' I explained. 'I'm not judging, I promise. But I love you and I'm worried about you.'

Lexi leaned back in the recliner and moved her sunglasses down, blocking me out. 'Guess we're just getting older, Shayzie. Growing up.'

I dropped the subject for now. It looked like my parents weren't the only ones hiding things from me.

'Hey, do you like my new red glasses?' Lexi bounced them up and down on her face. 'They were a Christmas gift from Aileen. She sent them all the way from London! I had no idea my big sister had such good taste.'

I reached across to grab them for a closer look. 'I love the union jack along the side. They go great with your bikini.'

She tossed her hair off her shoulder. 'They do match perfectly, don't they?'

'How many pairs of sunglasses is that now?' I asked.

She wrinkled her nose. 'Twenty-seven.'

'You know you have a problem, right?'

'I know.' She pouted. 'But I love 'em all and I can't stop buying them.'

The sound of a lawnmower next door interrupted our bonding session.

'I wonder if that's the hottie?' said Lexie. She crept across to the fence and pushed her face against the wood, peeking through the slats. 'It's him!'

She waved me over, but I stayed where I was. I was not interested

30

in another run in with that guy. Besides, if the rumours were true, he might be a criminal. Lexie watched him for a while through the slats, then started climbing the fence.

I jumped up. 'Lexi, what are you doing?' I tried to pull her down before she got his attention.

'Let go of me,' she said, kicking me away.

Lexi continued climbing and in no time had reached the top and perched herself up there. I didn't think there was much chance of her falling backwards today.

'Lexi! Get down,' I urged.

She ignored me and adjusted her bright red bikini top that showed off her tan. She flipped all her hair over one shoulder and waited for him to notice. It didn't take long before the lawnmower rumbled to silence. I crouched down low and tried to peek through a hole in the wood. There was no way I wanted him to see me.

Lexi waved. 'Hi there, neighbour, I'm Lexi.'

Tanned legs stopped just near my vision. 'Shouldn't you be wearing that thing in the water?'

Lexi threw her head back and laughed an exaggerated laugh. He probably had a pathetic grin plastered across his face.

'It's called a bikini and it works just as good from up here,' said Lexi.

I gagged at her flirting. She was so obvious sometimes! I could never speak to a guy like that. My mouth would dry up and no words would come out if I tried to be as casual as Lexi.

'When you finish mowing all that grass, I bet you'll be ... hot and sweaty,' said Lexi.

I cringed even more. *Just stop talking Lexi.*

'Well, my cousin ...' she looked pointedly at me. 'And I agreed that we should be neighbourly and invite you over for a swim.'

'Your cousin? Don't suppose she rides like a maniac on a purple bike?'

I bit my tongue, not wanting him to discover me squatted here.

'You should have seen her the other day,' he said. 'This chick thought she owned the road and nearly crashed right into my car.'

I couldn't let him get away with blaming it all on me. 'Hey, I'm not the maniac. You're the one who can't drive.' Immediately my fists clenched for giving myself away.

'Aww, is that you, Princess?'

His legs moved closer to the fence before dark eyes stared down at me. I stood up and moved back from the divide.

'Do you two know each other?' Lexi looked between us.

I shook my head.

'Yes,' he contradicted me.

I glared at the guy from next door. Three times I had spoken with him and each time he managed to be more infuriating than the last.

'We *don't* know each other,' I said. 'And don't call me *Princess*.'

'You know what, Lexi? I might take you up on your offer.' He kept his gaze on me as he spoke to her, as if daring me to withdraw the swim invitation.

Lexi pushed her chest out further. 'Come over whenever you're ready,' she said.

I scowled at them both. She made me sick with her flirting and he was just as nauseating.

'Thanks, neighbour, I'll do that. By the way I'm Callen.' He sent a wink my way, then disappeared from view.

The lawnmower began again and Lexi climbed down the fence. She crossed her arms and raised an eyebrow.

'What?' I walked back to the pool and plonked on the recliner.

Lexi stood in front of me, hands on hips. 'Well? What haven't you told me?'

'I don't know him, I promise.'

'He called you *Princess?*'

I rolled my eyes. 'I might have spoken to him, but only once, er, maybe twice.' I sighed. 'It's not what you think. We *do not* know each other and I don't want to get to know him.'

I looked at the blue water that was normally inviting, but today it teased me. No more delights to be enjoyed, just hidden threats beneath. Soon the neighbour from hell would be in it. He would be splashing and flirting with Lexi while she put on her charm. This swim was going to be trouble. The worst part was that there was nothing I could do to stop it.

Chapter 7

I peeled my sweaty bike shorts off and flung them on the ground. 'Urrggh.'

Then I sprayed on some deodorant, along with a squirt of perfume. At least I wouldn't stink. Not that I cared what the neighbour thought. I wriggled into my new bikini and caught a glimpse of my reflection. I paused at the mirror and tapped the empty space where my necklace should be. We looked and looked the other night but never found it. I turned sideways, sucked in my stomach and pushed my chest out. Who was I kidding? Lexi was blessed with a slim frame and curves where they were supposed to be. My body might be lean, but it lacked the femininity of Lexi's. I flattened the frizz behind my ears and looked closely at my face. Scattered freckles covered my nose and light blue eyes stared back.

I grabbed a towel from the laundry and joined Lexi in the backyard. She closed the magazine she was reading as I approached.

'Can't believe you still buy that magazine,' I said.

We used to devour the monthly, teenage-girl magazine when we started high school. It felt grown up, and a bit naughty to read the stories. They didn't shy away from tough topics! Mum always said I could ask her whatever I wanted, but no thanks. I would do anything to avoid the embarrassment of *that* conversation with her.

'I still like looking at the hairstyles and clothes,' she said, as she put the mag on the table and rolled on her side.

I sat down on the side of the pool. 'What does the good doctor advise this month?'

The sheer sarong that matched the bikini split across my leg. My tan could do with some work, but the skin I inherited rarely complied.

Lexi flicked through the pages until she found the right section. She read out loud, 'Dear Doctor, I haven't got my period yet. I'm 14. Is there something wrong with me? From Waiting.'

'Dear Waiting,' I said. 'Be glad you don't have your lady's days yet and stop complaining.'

'Ooh, here's another one,' said Lexi. 'Dear Doctor, I perspire a lot when I'm nervous. What can I do to stop this? From Sweaty.'

'It is *not* signed *Sweaty*.' I grabbed the magazine from her. 'Eww it is! Dear Sweaty, carry deodorant at all times, especially in case of an emergency heatwave.'

'We should go through my collection and read all the doctor questions now we're older and wiser,' said Lexi, with a wink.

'There's no way real people send that stuff in,' I said. 'They have to be making it up. *Sweaty? Waiting?* As if any of that's from real people!'

'You're probably right.' She closed the magazine and sat upright. 'Now listen up, Shayzie. You better be nice when our new *friend* comes over.'

'Humph! The guy's a psycho,' I said. 'You're the one who told us he beat up some guy.'

'*Allegedly* beat up some guy,' she clarified.

'Oh, now it's "allegedly", is it?'

'Don't believe everything you hear,' Lexi said, grinning.

'It was you I heard it from!'

She shrugged and adjusted herself so her perfect figure was on show.

Callen wouldn't know where to look. *Creeaakk.* The side gate opened.

'That's him so just be … polite,' said Lexi.

I could do that, especially when I didn't plan on talking to him. I dangled my legs in the pool and swirled my ankles around. A figure moved out the corner of my eye, but I refrained from looking up. I didn't want him to think I cared that he came over for a swim.

'Good afternoon, ladies.'

My eyes deceived me and looked up anyway, damn it. Callen sidled up alongside Lexi. She took her time sitting up which gave him the best opportunity to appreciate her trim, tanned body.

'So, you finally chopped all that grass to size and came to join us?' she said.

Callen settled on the lounge chair beside Lexi. 'Anything to keep Pop off my case.'

'Are you staying with him for the whole summer?' she asked.

'Something like that.' He looked away, avoiding Lexi's inquiring gaze.

I held my breath, hoping she didn't come right out and ask about the bashed guy. Subtlety and Lexi did not always go together. She opened her mouth, paused, then closed it. Phew! Dark eyes looked across the pool and caught me staring. I quickly looked away. Suddenly cold water hit my skin.

'Thought you might be missing your tennis ball,' he said.

I fought the urge to kick some water in his direction. He flicked some hair off his face, teasing me with the smirk playing on his lips. I pulled the ball from the water.

'Maybe you should keep it? You can work on those slow reflexes.' I tossed it back at him.

His hand flew up and caught it easily. 'My reflexes work fine, thanks.'

Grr! I stood up and removed my sarong, throwing it to the side of the pool. I dove into the clear water and the initial cold made my stomach clench. I stayed beneath the surface all the way to the end. Finally, I emerged and wiped the water from my eyes. Lexi was laughing at something.

'Hey, Shae, did you know Callen is a swimmer? He offered to give you some tips on that flop you just did.'

'At least it wasn't a belly whacker,' I teased. The whole family knew Lexi couldn't dive.

Callen leaned forward. 'Actually, it was a bit of a belly whacker.'

I thumped the water and a spray of water landed on both of them.

'Woah, you better watch yourself, Lexi. Your cousin has a bit of a temper.'

'Shae? No, she's a sweet, gentle thing,' Lexi crooned.

Callen laughed and stood up. He removed his t-shirt and tossed it aside. I looked away but took a moment too long and Lexi caught me.

'*I. Told. You,*' she mouthed.

I snuck another look then ducked under the water to cool my cheeks. I pushed off against the pool wall and glided to the end. I came up for air only to find Callen right beside me in the water. As he shook his head drops of water flicked my face.

'I could give you some tips if you like,' he said. 'I swam squad for a couple of years.'

'Think I'd rather stick with belly whackers.'

'Are you sure? I'd be happy to teach you,' he offered.

The confined space between us shrank and I couldn't seem to catch my breath. How dare he have this effect! I tried to speak, but my mouth was dry.

'No lessons needed thanks.' I cleared my throat. 'Although, I could give you some tips on driving. I actually know how to.'

He grinned, which only annoyed me more. I pushed against the edge and floated backwards, away from him.

'Shae, are you being nice to our guest?' asked Lexi as she jumped up and sashayed toward the edge of the water.

Callen slapped the water's surface spraying her with an arc of water. Her shrieks soon turned to giggles. I reached the other end of the pool and hauled myself out.

'I'll leave the both of you to it,' I said. Quickly, I grabbed a towel from the chair to wrap around myself and walked toward the back door.

'Can you grab some drinks to bring out?' Lexi called after me.

I glanced over my shoulder and caught Callen watching me. His lips were set in a straight line with a creased forehead, as though something had confused him. Lexi said I had to be polite and I was. I even managed not to yell at him. She never said anything about hanging around to help entertain him. It looked like she had that part covered all by herself.

Chapter 8

Inside the kitchen I rummaged through the fridge for some cans of soft drink. The back-door slid across and Lexi stepped inside.

'I'm gonna grab some chips,' she said.

I was about to scoop the drinks up when I saw my backpack leaning against the stool.

'Hey, did you know there was a letter for me?' I searched through the bag. 'It was left near the front door.'

'That's weird. Who's it from?'

I shrugged and pulled the yellow envelope out. There were no identifying features on the front and no return address. I tore open the top and found a folded A4 piece of white paper inside. It shook out easily.

The room closed in around me. 'Is this a joke?'

'What is it?' Lexi moved closer to look.

I turned the paper around and showed her the printed colour photograph. There was no mistaking the front view of my dad. The black cap might have covered his thinning hair, but it did nothing to hide his face squashed against another woman. It was hard to make out the woman from her side profile. I moved the picture closer for a better look, but it was too grainy.

'This was delivered here, in the mail?' Lexi passed the picture back. 'Who's the chick?'

'Not Mum, obviously,' I snapped.

A mix of fear and sympathy crossed her face. 'Do you recognise her?' Lexi asked.

Another closer look made little difference. The image was too blurred.

'Hey, there's something on the back,' said Lexi.

I flipped it over and found a handwritten note. *Shae, we need to talk. It's not what you think. Call me.* A mobile phone number was scrawled beneath the message.

The back door screeched open making me jump.

Callen appeared in the kitchen. He must have felt the tension as he looked between Lexi and I. It was obvious from our awkward silence he had walked in on something important.

'Is everything okay in here?' he asked.

Lexi looked at me and I nodded. 'Everything's great,' I said, staring at the sheet of paper that had just delivered some random message.

Lexi moved to the pantry and rustled around inside, apparently lost for words for once. My eyes flicked to Callen who was watching me closely.

'Are you sure you're, okay?' He stepped toward me. 'You look kind of pale.'

My head spun and I swayed forward. I slammed my hand on the note and slid it toward me. 'Like I said, everything's great.'

I disappeared down the hallway and clenched my fists to stop the shaking. Who the hell was Dad embracing? And even more importantly, did Mum know about it?

***

'Did you sleep okay?' Blake asked the next day.

'Not really,' I answered, honestly.

Sleep evaded me last night. Every time my eyes closed, the picture of Dad embracing that mystery woman filled the vacant space. When I finally fell asleep, I dreamt of faceless people who appeared out of nowhere and followed me along the street. Each time I turned around they disappeared like cold breath on a winter morning.

'Well, if you keep hanging out with Lexi you'll be sleeping in until lunchtime every day,' said Blake.

We both stayed up past midnight watching episodes of The Swamp. It was addictive viewing and those brothers were good looking!

My mobile phone trilled at a deafening volume and Blake snatched it up. 'Hel-lo!' He looked at me and smiled. 'Hey, Aunty Zan.'

I froze, even though I had been waiting for this call.

Blake nodded. 'Yep, I'll put her on.'

He shoved the phone in my face. I grabbed it hesitantly and mustered up a smile, even though she couldn't see me.

'Hi, Mum.'

'Shae! How are you sweetheart?' she asked.

'I'm fine.' My pitch was unnaturally high and I tried to stay calm. It's not like Mum could have known about the letter I got showing Dad and some random woman.

'I wanted to check in and make sure you were having fun.'

I turned away from Blake. 'Yeah, of course I'm having fun.'

'I haven't got long. I'm in between meetings.'

'Where's Dad?' My voice cracked on the question.

'Your father? Why?' Her voice sounded muffled.

'It's just that I haven't spoken to him yet,' I said.

The silence stretched out between us. My stomach twisted waiting for her response as the printed image in the mail played on repeat in my mind.

'Actually, your father isn't here, Shae.'

'What do you mean he's not there?' I tried not to panic. 'Where is he?' The printed picture began to morph into a video in my head as Dad and the mystery woman ran toward each other and embraced.

'I mean, he's not in Airlie Beach. He had to go away for a few days.'

I tried to justify his absence. It could be a legitimate reason. Dad did travel to meet with his bigger accounting clients at times. But he never travelled over summer.

'Where's he gone?' I imagined Dad's things cleared out from his wardrobe. The coat hangers stripped of his suits and shirts. His toiletries removed out from the bathroom.

'Sorry sweetie, I can't talk for long.'

'*Mum.*' My voice was panicked.

'Be reasonable, Shae. I have to go. I'll call you back later tonight.'

Beep, beep, beep. The dial tone echoed in my ear.

'What was all that about?' Blake said.

Lexi joined us in the kitchen and took one look at my face before asking, 'What's happened?'

'That was Mum. She said Dad's gone away.' I raised an eyebrow.

'What's wrong with that?' Blake said. 'Doesn't he always go away?'

'Yeah, he does, it's just strange for this time of year,' I explained.

'Strange because he didn't say anything and our little Shae needs to know everything,' said Lexie, trying to make light of the situation.

'You two are weird.' Blake adjusted his hat and left the kitchen.

'*Be reasonable, Shae.*' She can't be serious. I'm always the understanding daughter, especially when her work gets in the way. As the personal assistant to the owner of Levelled Architects & Co, Mum's regularly left to deal with everything. That's meant missing things she had already committed to with me and I've never complained.

A conversation from a couple of weeks ago resurfaced.

'*You started this, not me!*' Mum said.

'*Be reasonable. You know I never meant to hurt you.*'

42

'Be reasonable? You must be joking. I've only ever been reasonable.'

'Susannah, you know this was not supposed to happen,' said Dad. 'It wasn't part of the agreement we made.'

'Well, it's too late now,' said Mum.

That was all I heard before she slammed the front door and left. I didn't know what Dad started or why Mum was meant to be reasonable. I was beginning to think the picture of Dad and another woman embracing had something to do with it.

'I might go for a ride,' I said.

Lexi looked up, surprised. 'Do you want me to come?'

'Nah, I just think some fresh air will help clear my head.'

Outside I got my bike from the shed and did the mandatory wheel checks, only to discover the back one was flat. I grabbed the pump, but the air hissed back out.

I stomped on the ground. 'Damn it!'

I really needed to burn off some of this tension, but I couldn't fix the puncture because I hadn't bought a replacement from the last flat. Grr! I spotted Lexi's bike shoved up in the back corner. It probably hadn't been used since the last time I stayed. I dragged it out and wiped off the dust and cobwebs. A few pumps of air in the tyres and it was good to go. I rolled down the driveway before I noticed a dark green car blocking the driveway and squeezed the brakes on.

The windows were tinted making the driver unidentifiable, but they were watching me through the window, that much I could tell. The engine revved a couple of times before the car took off. It swerved into the lane without indicating. The car behind blared its horn and skidded, but the Commodore was already long gone. Could the driver have been delivering another message for me? I quickly checked the letterbox, but it was empty. I immediately felt stupid. This whole thing with my parents was making me paranoid.

Chapter 9

After the flat tyre earlier, the rest of the day passed without incident. The street lights would be on soon, but the growing darkness didn't bother me as I walked along the footpath. The evening sky continued to change with shades of pink, white and purple. It reminded me of a bowl of trifle, my favourite dessert. My aunt and uncle were at a charity dinner for Motor Neurone Disease and both my cousins were working. That left me home alone tonight with my newly purchased tyre repair kit.

I didn't know whether to look forward to the solitude ahead or to dread it. At least on my own I wouldn't have to pretend everything was normal. Although, with company my mind was occupied. It wasn't chasing the same questions around and around. *We need to talk.* Four little words that threatened my world like nothing else. Who needed to talk? Did the woman in the picture send me the letter? How did she know where I was staying? Was she following me? I remembered the car at the end of the driveway with tinted windows. Did the driver deliver the envelope?

The phone number scribbled on the back of the picture was scorched into my brain. I had entered it into my phone a dozen times already, but each time something stopped me from pressing the green connect button.

A car passed and flicked on their headlights. I suddenly realised how dark it had become and picked up my pace as my shopping bag bounced beside me. My parents would flip out if they knew I was walking the street on my own at night. A scrappy dog ran toward the fence. Its high-pitched bark made me jump.

'Hello little puppy,' I said.

The little head popped above the white pickets as it bounded all the way along the property line.

When I was ten, I desperately wanted a dog. I begged my parents for weeks. Eventually Mum borrowed a friend's dog for a trial. The first couple of days were exciting, but after bathing, feeding, brushing and picking up its crap for a week, I lost all interest in having a dog and never brought up the idea again.

As I passed Mr. Sampson's driveway the headlights from Callen's car shone bright against the garage. Maybe he was coming back outside? The closed front door suggested otherwise. Oh well, not my problem. The last thing I needed was a barrage of sarcastic comments from that guy. The events from the last 24 hours were spinning in my head. I didn't need him to rile me up further so I continued past the house.

I knew there was only one way to stop the questions swirling around. Afraid I might stop myself, I quickly pulled out my phone and dialled the memorised number. It went straight to the automated voice message. I sighed, disappointed or relieved I wasn't sure?

I made my way toward my bike with the tyre tube I'd bought. The luminous glow of the car headlights next door captured my attention. Should I go next door and say something? If the lights stayed on, he'd have a flat battery tomorrow. Starting the day on a low was not a good way to begin, even for somebody as annoying as Callen.

'Damn it.' I trudged next door hoping Mr. Sampson answered.

I could tell him about the lights, he'd pass on the message and I would be on my way. Simple. My sense of obligation would be fulfilled and everyone could go about their business.

With a quick three raps on the door, I angled myself to flee from the steps. I was about to knock again, hand poised mid-air, when Callen answered. He wore only board shorts which was not what I was expecting. I stared at his bare torso. Thrown by his appearance I looked away, but not before a blush warmed my cheeks. Why couldn't I be more like Lexi and not flame at a half-naked guy? Callen crossed his arms and leant against the door undeterred by my embarrassment. This made my cheeks heat further.

An amused look pulled at his lips. 'What a pleasant surprise.'

'I'm sure it is.'

He took a step toward me. 'You wanna come inside?'

His voice was husky and I mustered all my strength to keep my face looking bored.

'Your headlights are on,' I said.

The smirk slipped from his face. 'What?'

'Your car. You know the big metal thing out the front with rubber wheels? The headlights are still on. So, unless you want a flat battery, you might want to turn them off.'

Callen looked past me. Annoyance flashed across his face and he moved back inside creating some much-needed space between us.

'Umm, okay … thanks,' he mumbled.

I turned to leave.

'Wait!' He grabbed my arm. 'What's going on?'

'What do you mean?' I looked at the restraint on my arm and shook it off. 'There's nothing going on, why?'

'Are you sure there's no prank waiting behind the car for me?' he asked.

I crossed my arms. 'Are you serious? I have better things to do than spend my time thinking of ways to prank you.'

'You're sure there's no Lexi ready to throw flour bombs over me?'

he continued.

'What? No! You're unbelievable. I come over to do the right thing and you accuse me of doing something stupid.'

'All right, I'm sorry. Calm down.' He pushed his hair back from his face. 'I am sorry. That was dumb of me to think that.'

'I just didn't want you to start the day …' I stopped before I revealed too much. 'I just thought you should know.'

Callen studied me. I held his gaze, even though I was wilting under the intensity.

'Then I suppose I should thank you for your kind deed,' he said.

I waited, but he just looked confused. 'Go on then,' I said.

He grinned and bowed his head, understanding what I was waiting for. 'Thank you.'

'Whatever.' I ran down the steps and along the driveway.

I knew he was watching me, but I didn't look back. Instead, I dragged my bike out from where it was dumped this morning. Mr. Sampson's front wire door creaked followed by a thud. I peeked across the low fence as Callen walked toward his car. I noticed he had covered up with a singlet. I continued dragging my bike from the garage determined to fix the tyre. I looked over again as the interior light came on. Callen bent down and flicked the driving lights off. Our eyes met and I was the first to look away. The car door slammed, but I didn't hear the front door again.

I tried to remove the punctured tyre that helped to ruin my day.

'Do you need a hand?' Callen's voice cut through the silent night air.

I ignored his offer and kept trying. It was stuck, so I pulled harder. Finally, it wrenched off and I flung it on the front lawn. As I stood up my head connected with the windowsill. *Whack!* I slid down to the step clutching my head.

Callen appeared by my side. 'Are you okay?'

A groan escaped and I bit my lip to stop another one.

'Come on, I'll help you inside,' he said.

'I don't need your help,' I said, through clenched teeth.

He took a step back but didn't walk away. I glared at him. I hated that he had seen me in a moment of weakness. I tried to stand up straight, to prove it was no more than a bump, but dizziness overwhelmed me and I fell forward.

Callen caught me. 'Whoah, easy there.'

I tried to push him away. 'Let me go.'

'Stop fighting and let me help. You need ice on the bump.'

My strength faded and I didn't resist as he guided me inside. The world was spinning around me. Callen supported my body with his arm tucked around my waist. I gave in and let him help, too dizzy to walk on my own.

'Sit down,' he said.

My head throbbed as the cupboard doors slammed and the ice rattled from the freezer. Callen scooped some on to the tea-towel and moved toward the table where I was supporting my swollen head. He moved my hand aside and gently placed the ice on top. I winced from the pain. The chill spread and sent ripples down my spine.

'It'll hurt for a bit, but you gotta keep it there until it settles down.' His voice was gentle. 'Trust me, I've had plenty of knocks from rugby.'

'That explains a few things,' I grumbled.

After a while the cold numbed the throbbing and the pain did ease, just like Callen said it would. I realised he was still holding the tea towel with the ice. I reached up and my hand moved over his. Our fingers met and neither one of us pulled away.

'I got it,' I said, my voice shaky.

Slowly he withdrew his hand from beneath mine. He stepped back, giving me some space. His body remained tense, flexed.

Worried maybe? I tried to push the stupid notion aside. He thought I was a primped up little princess, so why would he be worried? Yet his dark eyes watched me, intense and unflinching. This time it was not the cold ice that made me tingle.

Chapter 10

Tick, tick, tick. The kitchen clock marked each passing second. This was not how I imagined my evening would play out. Alone at home, yes. Alone with Callen, no.

'Do you want a drink?' he asked.

'Yes please, and something for the throbbing.'

He turned toward a cupboard, paused, then changed direction. I waited to see if he would ask for help, but he didn't.

'The cupboard above the fridge,' I directed him.

He found some paracetamol and placed it in front of me with the water. One lone drip trickled down the side and pooled at the base.

'Thanks.' I swallowed the pain relief hoping it would kick in soon.

My neck was stiff as I tried to sit up. It must have gotten jarred when I cracked my head. Once Dad had to wear a neck brace for three weeks. He never complained even though it must have been uncomfortable, especially in the North Queensland heat.

Callen joined me at the table. He played a short rhythm on the table with his fingertips. *Tappity, tap, tap. Tap, tap.*

'How do you feel, Princess?'

He reverted to his moniker for me. This time there was no malice to it. Instead, the reference was almost friendly, caring.

'Shae. My name's Shae.'

His chair scraped against the tiles. 'How do you feel, *Shae*?'

'My head is pounding,' I said.

'You better not go to sleep then because you might have a concussion.' He tapped out the rhythm again. 'You might not wake up.'

'You'd like that wouldn't you?' I said.

'Hey, you saved me from a flat battery and I saved you from collapsing in the driveway. I'd say we're even,' he said.

'Good, I wouldn't want to owe you anything.'

Callen shrugged. 'Why did you tell me about the headlights really?'

'I told you why.'

'But I thought you would have enjoyed seeing me in trouble in the morning.'

'Do you really think I'm that heartless?' I asked, angry with him again.

'No, that's not what I meant.' He crossed his arms. 'I think you might be far from it.' He watched me, studying me intently. Waiting for a response.

'It's been a rough twenty-four hours,' I said.

Callen leaned back in the kitchen chair. 'Geez, I'd love to know what you call rough.'

'Let's just say that you caught me at a weak moment.'

That was as much as I planned to explain to him tonight. I didn't even mean to tell him that, but the small space between us was intense and it slipped out.

I reached for my necklace and remembered it was still missing. 'Damn it.'

'Does it hurt?' He asked, his face serious.

'No, it's my necklace. I lost it around here somewhere the other day and it still hasn't turned up.'

Callen pulled himself upright. 'What does this necklace look like?'

51

I explained the blue stone and his eyes darted toward his house.

'My dad gave it to me for my sixteenth birthday,' I said.

'That makes it pretty special then, huh?'

'Yeah, it is to me.'

'It sucks when you lose something important to you,' Callen said in a low voice, almost whispering.

I couldn't help thinking we were talking about two different things.

'Do you want to talk about your *rough* twenty-four hours? Hair straightener wouldn't work?' Callen teased, filling the awkward silence that stretched out between us.

The photo in the mail came to mind. It would be good to talk to someone with no bias toward my situation. Somehow, I didn't think Callen was that person. He was confusing me with the two sides to him that I had seen. My first encounter was with a hot head that nearly ran me over, then tonight he was softer, almost gentle toward me.

My mask slipped, but only for a moment before I set it back in place. Perhaps this was his style. Lure the girl in then squeeze her back out. Lexi said he wouldn't be my type and she was right.

'Don't pretend you care about me,' I said.

His eyes narrowed at my tone. 'Don't worry, I don't.' He shoved the chair back and stood up, towering over me.

I flinched and pain flooded my forehead. 'Oww.'

It felt like needles being jammed into my face and skull. I held my head until it settled. I looked up at Callen. His face was scrunched in confusion, hurt.

He ran his hand through his hair. 'I better go.'

I stood up, trying to still the tremor that ran along my arms. I removed the tea towel and dropped it on the table.

'Oh wow.' Callen reached across to my head.

I moved my hand to block him. He stopped short of touching

my hair and jerked his hand back. My fingers ran over the lump bulging from my skull.

'Are you going to be alright on your own?' Concern laced his words and I couldn't help but feel guilty for my sharp response a moment ago.

I took a deep breath before replying. 'I'll be fine.'

'You need to keep the ice on longer,' he said, as he walked past me.

A sweet scent wafted over me, a combination of soap and musk. Footsteps trailed down the hallway before the front door clicked closed.

I collapsed back in the chair and it was then that I let the tears fall. They had been threatening to break free all day. Puddles formed on the table from the downfall, but like a sun shower it passed quickly, as though it never happened.

I dragged myself away from the table and stripped off naked in the bathroom. The room quickly filled with steam. The scalding water burnt my body as it pounded against my back. I rested my head against the tiles and watched the water chase itself down the drain. I lost track of how long I had been standing in the shower. It was long enough for the water to become cold. I turned the taps off and wrapped the fluffy white towel around me, shivering. It was a warm night though and didn't take long before the shivers passed. I dried my hair, being extra careful not to push against the lump. The pain in my head had subsided and I managed to get dressed into my pyjamas without any dizziness.

I remembered my bike abandoned out the front and groaned. I just wanted to climb into bed and curl up. But I didn't want anyone to drive over my bike when they got home. I tried to block out Callen, my parents, and that photograph from my mind. Instead, I concentrated on the task ahead. I slipped on my dressing gown and plodded toward the front door. It shouldn't take long then I could go to bed before anyone got home. I would tell them I turned in early because I had a headache. It was mostly the truth anyway.

The warm night air hit me as I opened the door and green tree frogs croaked in the garden nearby. I stepped outside and froze. My bike was leaning upright on its stand. The new tube had been replaced with the tyre attached. I squeezed the rubber between my fingers. It had been pumped up firmly, but not overdone. I looked next door knowing exactly who had fixed it. The knowledge left me grateful but confused. He didn't have to do that. I didn't ask for his help. I wrapped my arms around my middle. Damn it! This meant I owed him after all.

Chapter 11

The next day I dumped my shopping bags beside the wooden bench seat and slumped down. Thank goodness Lexi's shift was just about over. My feet couldn't take any more shopping. Mum and Dad had put a sizeable amount of guilt money into my account before they dropped me off, and I just gave it a good workout with the Christmas sales. Those half price leather sandals should look great with the bargain, aqua coloured singlet I bought.

It was easy to kill some time browsing while Lexi bagged up people's groceries. It also distracted me from my encounter with Callen last night, as well as the mystery photo. I tried calling the number this morning but got the message bank again. This time I left a message. *It's Shae.* I figured that's all I needed to say for now. *'We need to talk.'* That message on the note was driving me insane thinking about what it meant. I hoped the person who sent it called soon. I didn't understand why they would send the picture then wait to fill in the blanks. If they were so keen to make contact, they should just do it already.

I leant back on the chair and touched the lump on my head. It had settled down from last night, but it was still tender. At least the headache had gone away. Callen's concerned face made the nerves jangle inside my stomach. I was really rude to him when all he did was try to help me. He was kind and caring last night, not taunting and menacing. Which personality was his true one? Did I even want to find out? I dropped my face into my hands and rubbed my forehead. The guy was confusing me and I didn't want him in my thoughts. Except now he was right in the middle of them.

I looked up and noticed a girl watching me. She was only a little bit older than me, but she didn't look away when I locked eyes with hers. She stared as though she knew me. As though she was waiting for me to recognise her, but there was nothing familiar about her. After a while she stepped to the side and out of view. I continued watching the space and soon enough, she moved back into view and started to walk toward me. I racked my brain but couldn't place her face. Maybe she was friends with Lexi or Blake and I'd forgotten we met once.

'Shae!'

I turned toward the deep voice and saw Simon and Kai as they snaked their way through the shopping centre in my direction.

'Hey, how are ya?' Simon asked, grinning.

Kai lifted his chin in greeting. That was probably the most interaction I would get from him. There was no apology from him about the other day and his 'slip' into the water. He thought the whole thing was hilarious and continued to say so long after it was clearly not funny. I didn't know why Lexi bothered with him.

I looked back toward where the girl stood, but she had disappeared. I couldn't help feeling disappointed not knowing who she was.

'Been shopping?' Simon sat next to me.

I nodded. 'Lots of bargains! Hey, thanks for the other day at the Weir.'

He shrugged. 'No problem.'

Simon had sat with me until I was ready to walk off the Weir. He didn't rush me or make me feel stupid because of my fear of heights. Instead, he entertained me with funny stories about being an army kid and moving all the time. Like the time he left a whoopee cushion on the teacher's chair. Everyone knew he'd put it there and that made him the most popular kid at school afterwards.

A whizz of blonde hair flew past me and crashed into Kai.

'Hello, beautiful,' said Kai.

Lexi threw her head back and allowed him to pash her. My eyes met Simon's and he poked his finger down his throat pretending to gag. When she came up for air, Lexi pulled her hair out of the elastic constraints. She flicked it about and I was envious of the way it fell into position so easily. My hair always stayed stiff from being held back for so long. It was hard to tell it had even been released some days, even after the band was removed.

Lexi spotted my bags and rifled through them. 'What did you buy? Anything for me?'

'Hey!' I snatched the bags from her. 'You can borrow some things.'

She pouted.

'Maybe I did buy you something,' I said.

She clapped her hands like a little kid on their birthday.

I dug around inside the bags until I found the new pair of sunglasses. 'Here you go, to add to your collection.'

'Thanks, Shayzie, I love them.'

The black frames covered half her face. They looked great on her of course.

'Come on, let's get out of here,' said Kai, grabbing Lexi's hand.

Simon and I followed behind. He talked about some roller-skating disco night coming up. I tried to look interested, but roller-skating and I didn't mix very well.

'You and Lexi should come. Kai would like that and so would I.' He smiled and I again ignored the urge to push against the dent in his chin.

I tried even harder to ignore the message in his invitation, so I made up an excuse instead. 'It's probably not a great idea. I'm not the most balanced person on four wheels.'

'Come on, it will be fun,' he urged.

My eyes narrowed. 'I think we might have different ideas about fun.'

We continued walking through the shopping centre. I looked around, only to settle on a pair of dark eyes I knew well. Callen leant against a shop window and watched our group walk by. His look was guarded, annoyed almost. Lexi threw him a big wave and started to detour toward him, but Kai grabbed her wrist and pulled against it.

She scowled and tried to shrug out of his grip. 'Hi, Callen,' she called out instead.

He didn't return the greeting, instead he stood upright with fists clenched and walked our way.

'Don't bother talking to him,' Kai said. 'The guy's a waste of space.'

'What's your problem with Callen?' Lexi asked.

'Nothing, I just wanna get out of here.' He pulled on her arm and dragged her away from an advancing Callen.

I stayed still while Simon shoved his hands in his pockets and waited with me.

'Wasn't Lexi allowed to stop and talk?' Callen asked.

I shrugged. 'Guess not. Do you know Kai?'

He ignored my question and reached across, pausing halfway before dropping his hand. 'How's your head?'

'A bit sore, but I'll live.'

Simon bounced next to me with a nervous energy. If the two knew each other, neither let on. But if Kai knew who Callen was, it made sense Simon would know him as well.

'I better get going,' I said.

Callen nodded and moved out of my way.

I walked past then spun back around to look at him. 'Hey,

thanks for fixing my bike. You didn't have to do that.'

'It didn't take long, besides, now we're even,' he said.

'I thought we already were?'

He shrugged and walked away in the opposite direction.

Simon and I kept moving through the plaza. He must know something about Kai and Callen. Perhaps the rumours were true and Callen did beat up someone Kai knew.

'Did you know that guy back there?' I asked.

'Not as well as Kai.'

'What do you mean? How does Kai know him?' I tried to keep my tone light.

Simon sighed. 'I don't really know that guy Callen. But I know about him.'

'So, *what* do you know of him?'

'Let's just say I wouldn't mention him around Kai. His sister—'

'What are you two whispering about?' Lexi asked, blocking the exit from the plaza.

'Wouldn't you like to know?' I pushed Lexi out through the automatic doors and she ran to catch up with Kai.

I started to follow just as Simon tugged me back from the pedestrian crossing. My neck jerked and a pain shot through my head like last night.

'Slow down, idiot!' Simon called after the car that flew past.

My heart pounded. One more step and it would have hit me. It already had a dinted rear end. Driving carefully probably wasn't their style.

'Are you okay?' Simon grabbed my hand.

'I didn't even see it,' I said, eyes wide.

'I know. It nearly collected you right up! It came out of nowhere.'

I looked down at Simon who was still holding my hand. He waited a moment before letting go.

'Come on!' Lexi yelled out, oblivious to my near-death experience.

We tried crossing the road again. I checked both ways this time and managed to cross unscathed. I followed Lexi toward Kai's car in the parking space. I was about to get in when I saw the car that nearly hit me. It was idling a couple of rows across. The tinted windows made it impossible to see inside. If I didn't know any better, I would have thought the driver was watching us.

Chapter 12

The music pumped loudly inside the car as we cruised along the Townsville waterfront known as the *Strand*. Palm trees lined the foreshore while walkers, joggers and bike riders controlled the walkway. The muggy, summer heat made the air feel thicker than normal. All the windows were wound down, but the breeze was hot and not at all cooling. I wanted the creature comfort of air conditioning. Why didn't Kai turn it on? His fancy car had it.

He drove the full length of the waterfront towards Kissing Point, the fortification structure with a long, rich, military history that overlooked the watery entrance to Townsville. Eventually Kai pulled into a car park near the rock pool. We used to come here all the time as kids. The stinger nets went up from November to May. Once Dale was showing off and went outside the enclosure with his friends. He didn't want to, but he couldn't back down with his mates watching. He got stung by a box jellyfish and was doused with vinegar to neutralise the sting. When the lifeguards arrived, they peeled back each tentacle that had suctioned itself to his thigh. It was so bad that he got a ride in the ambulance and the nickname Stinger afterwards.

Kai cut the engine but left the keys in the ignition. 'Wait here,' he ordered, then slammed the door behind him.

Lexi turned the music off and faced backwards from the front seat. 'We haven't got much time. Spill everything you know, Simon.'

'About what?'

'What's the deal with Kai and Callen?' she asked.

Simon shuffled uncomfortably in his seat. 'What is it with you chicks and that guy?'

'He's our new neighbour,' said Lexi.

'Really?'

'Well, for a little while. I think we have a right to know as much about him as we can.'

'Why don't you just ask Kai?' he said.

'I did and he won't tell me anything.' She pouted.

'Well, there you go. There's nothing you need to worry about then.'

'What do you know, Simon?' I asked, interested, cautious.

He sighed and clasped his hands on top of his head. 'Oh fine, but you *cannot* tell him that I told you.'

Lexi and I held our ring fingers up at the same time. We burst out laughing at the private joke then quickly became serious again, unsure how much time we had until Kai returned.

'You know Kai has a sister called Sondra?'

We nodded, even though I didn't know that.

'She went out with Callen for a while. Kai hated it because he was sure Callen was only using Sondra, which it turned out he was. Kai went ballistic and swore to make him pay, but it wasn't Callen who paid.'

'Are we ready?' Kai stuck his head through the window.

A guilty silence filled the car before Lexi turned around. Kai climbed inside and his gaze met mine in the rear-view mirror. I cut away to look out the window and tried to process what Simon said. Callen went out with Kai's sister. The bracelet I found from next door had *Sondra* engraved on it. It was too much of a coincidence, it had to be hers.

'Did you get some?' Simon asked.

'Get what?' asked Lexi.

'You'll see,' said Kai, running a finger along her collarbone.

Kai navigated the car out of the traffic as we headed away from the Strand. We passed a sign saying *Castle Hill*. As soon as the car started to wind its way upwards, I knew that's where we were headed. We passed a few brave people making the hike by foot up the mountain. It was a popular spot with multiple trails intersecting the hill. I tried the *Goat Track* once and my legs took an hour to stop shaking afterwards. I stared out the window and tried not to focus on anything. I didn't usually vomit, but the nausea that came with winding roads left my stomach unsettled. I breathed deep and wriggled my toes.

'Are you okay?' Simon asked.

'It'll pass, don't worry.' I forced a smile.

He offered me a water bottle, which I accepted gratefully. After a while we made it to the top of the look-out. The car park was deserted at this time of the afternoon. We got out and made our way toward one of the viewing platforms. It was a bit of a hike, but it offered a great view of Magnetic Island. I leant against the safety rail to take in the fresh air.

'Don't tell me you still get car sick?' said Lexi.

'You better not spew in my car,' said Kai. 'My dad will kill me.'

'I won't throw up, and thanks for caring,' I said, with sarcasm.

Lexi wrapped her arm around me. 'Oh, honey, are you feeling sick?'

'Get away.' I shoved her backward and moved toward the right side of the platform for a different view. You could see the swimming pools in backyards from up here.

'I think I see our house,' said Lexi.

'Oh really, where is it?' I nudged her.

'It's just over there. Or is that way?' She screwed up her face.

'Well, it's there somewhere!'

Kai moved closer to Lexi and nuzzled her neck. I watched as he pulled a packet of cigarettes out of his pocket. He lit one before offering the packet to Lexi. Her eyes darted to me before accepting the offered gift. She didn't bother to offer me one, instead she threw the packet to Simon. He caught it, but didn't take one.

'Don't let me stop you,' I said.

Simon looked down, but still didn't take one. Kai watched on and I could tell Simon was weighing things up. Impress Kai. Or impress me. Kai snatched the packet back from Simon, making his decision easy.

'You're such a downer sometimes,' Kai said, shaking the packet of smokes in front of Simon's face. The grotesque image to deter smokers with the caption *Smoking causes throat cancer* stared back at him.

Simon slapped his hand away. 'Shut up, I just don't feel like one.'

I had no idea how often Simon normally smoked. I didn't see him smoking the other day at the Weir. And Lexi only seemed to smoke around certain people. Did that mean she was a social smoker now?

'What about you, Shae, do you want one?' Kai teased, knowing exactly what my response would be. 'Don't overthink it and maybe live a bit.'

'Don't think those things will help much with the living part,' I said.

He dragged on his cigarette and blew the smoke toward me. I looked at Lexi, questioningly. She leant to one side with her arms drawn tight around her stomach. She stayed quiet, averting her gaze. Maybe this was how she spent her weekends now. Hanging out in bushes and taking smokes off this loser.

'I like being in charge of what goes in my body. I have my own *mind*.'

I looked pointedly at Lexi. Who was this mouse letting some guy dictate to her and make decisions for her? It sure wasn't the Lexi I knew.

I turned away from the viewing platform and walked back toward the car. A bench faced the opposite view so I sat there. There were heaps of places I'd rather be right now, but instead I was stuck here. Hanging out with Lexi and her boyfriend did not seem to go well for me. That was going to be tricky if I was staying with Lexi for most of the summer holidays.

Simon walked over and sat down beside me. 'He was just being a smart arse, you know that right?'

'I don't really care what Kai thinks,' I said, keeping my eyes on the view ahead. I could see the Ross River curling through the town from this angle.

'What about me? Do you care what I think?'

I turned to look at him, surprised by the question. 'That depends. Can you think for yourself, or do you let Kai do all the thinking for you?'

Simon grabbed his heart as though I just stabbed him. 'Oh, you're harsh. You're killing me, Shae.'

I pushed him off me, laughing as he doubled over moaning.

'Seriously, Simon. Why do you hang out with him? I keep asking Lexi the same thing, except she just makes excuses for him.'

Simon's knee bounced in time with his chewing. His gum popped making a quiet cracking sound.

'I can think for myself. I *do* think for myself. But sometimes when you move around as much as me, well, you get sick of always trying to fit in. Sometimes it's easier to just go with the flow.'

'I can understand that, but what if the flow is against what you really want?'

He sighed. 'It's hard being the new kid all the time, Shae. Starting over … again and again. I know I told you it's not that bad, but it kind of sucks.'

I smiled. 'Don't be so hard on yourself. You're a great guy.'

He looked up, surprised. 'You think so?' He moved to face me better.

'Of course! What I mean is that you don't need anyone else's approval. Especially someone like Kai.'

'Ah, but you're wrong. I kind of owe Kai. He stuck up for me on my first day at school. Took me under his wing and showed me around. Geez, the first time I went to his house I couldn't believe it. The place is a mansion! You know his parents are filthy rich right?'

Lexi hadn't mentioned it but maybe that's why she liked him? I wouldn't have thought my cousin was shallow about materialistic things like that.

'I didn't keep hanging out with him because of the money if that's what you're thinking. His dad never gives him any of it anyway. But it was good to have someone to hang out with and somewhere to go, instead of home,' said Simon. 'Home can be … a little rough sometimes.'

I waited for more of an explanation, but he didn't offer anything. Instead, he leaned back against the seat. He took my hand and for some reason I let him. I guess we all had secrets we had to live with. My life was filling up with them from the people around me. Lexi, Callen, my parents and now Simon. Some support from a friend was the least I could offer him.

Chapter 13

The next morning my mobile phone rang from the bedroom. I raced toward the noise, but it stopped buzzing just as I reached for it. It was the same number I had been calling from the anonymous letter. What game were they playing?

A knock at the front door startled me. I held on to the phone and rushed down the hallway to answer it. My eyes widened at the unexpected visitor.

'Hi,' said Callen.

His hair was wet, as though he had just showered. His sweet and soapy scent swept past me. It was the same musk smell as the other night.

My nerves kicked up a notch and I wasn't sure what to say. I tried to crack a joke to cover my lost ability to speak. 'Have I left my bike lights on?'

'Ha, funny, I like it.'

There was an awkward pause that I waited for him to fill, but he didn't.

'Hey, about what I said the other night, the whole pretending to care comment. I shouldn't have said that—'

'Forget about it,' he interrupted me. 'You were hurt. It doesn't matter.'

I stepped onto the porch. 'It does matter and I'm sorry.'

I waited for Callen to look at me so he could see I meant it, but when he did, I began to crumble from the intensity. I think I really hurt his feelings.

Callen stepped away from me, giving me some much-needed breathing room. 'I was just on my way out, but I wanted to talk to you. Alone,' he said.

My skin prickled at the idea of being alone with Callen again. I tried to quash the effect he had on me. I closed the door and moved further out onto the porch. Callen pulled something out from his pocket and dangled a silver chain in front of me.

'Where did you get that?' I snatched it from him.

'I'm guessing that's the missing necklace from your dad?'

'Yes!' I threw my arms around him without thinking, grateful for its return. His body tensed and I quickly stepped away. 'Sorry, I didn't mean to do that.'

A smile crept up his face as he watched me, missing nothing. Oh yeah, he knew the effect he had on me.

'I can't believe you found it,' I said. 'Thank you.'

'I saw it mowing the lawn the other day. How did you lose it in my pop's yard?'

I tried to think about how that could have happened, and then I remembered Lexi's turtle pose. It must have come off the day she fell over the fence, but if I told him that story she would kill me.

'I didn't know it was yours until you mentioned it the other night,' he explained.

My body responded to the memory of how he helped me with the ice. I tried to clasp the necklace around my neck.

'Do you want some help?' He reached for the necklace and I turned around.

I pulled my curly hair to the side and pushed some wispy bits out of the way. My heart rate accelerated at his touch.

'There you go.' His hands rested softly on my shoulders, then they were gone.

'Thanks.' I turned back to face him.

Somehow, we were closer than before and my breath hitched. The blue stone was heavy against my skin.

'It looks nice. Matches your eyes.' He pushed a wisp of hair off my cheek.

My mobile rang, cutting through the charged atmosphere. The screen showed the same number as before.

'I have to answer this,' I said.

Callen turned away, giving me some privacy.

'Hello?'

The other end remained silent.

'Who is this?'

The person disconnected from me.

'Must have been a wrong number,' I lied.

'I better get going.' He checked his watch. 'Damn, I'm already late.'

'Late for what?' I asked.

He shuffled uncomfortably. 'Late for … a lesson in life.' He walked toward his car.

I waved goodbye as he backed out from the driveway. He honked the horn as he drove off down the street. I shook my head at the cryptic explanation, *a lesson in life*. That could mean just about anything. My phone buzzed and I dropped the thing on the wooden decking. The same number as before flashed on the screen.

I snatched it up from the ground. 'Hello?'

Again, there was no answer from the other end.

My voice rose. 'Is someone there?' I could tell there was. 'You have three seconds before I hang up. One, two—'

'Is this Shae Dowinger?' a female voice asked.

'Who wants to know?'

'I'm sorry for hanging up before. I chickened out when you answered. I mean I wanted to speak with you except then I panicked when I heard your voice. Did you get my letter?'

After the rambling, the mention of the letter got my full attention.

'You know I got it, otherwise I wouldn't have called you,' I answered.

'I'm sorry to be secretive like I have been, but it had to be this way. I needed you to see the photo so you'd believe me.'

'Who the hell are you and what do you want?'

'It's complicated,' she said, almost a whisper.

'Did you take that picture, or are you the woman in the photo?' I asked.

There was a scratching sound before I heard another muffled voice.

'Hello, are you still there?' I asked.

'I'm sorry, I gotta go. I'll call you back later and we can arrange to meet,' the mystery caller said.

'No! Tell me now.'

'I promise I'll tell you everything, just not over the phone.'

Tears prickled and I blinked to hold them back. There was a person on the end of the phone who could give me the answers I wanted. Or at least some of them.

'Don't call me, Shae, I'll call you. Soon, I promise.'

Two promises later and she disconnected from me. Cut the connection just like that! And I still knew nothing more than I did before the call. I slipped to the floor staring at the screen.

My thumb moved to press the call button and ring her back, but I didn't. Instead, I curled up into a ball. I went back over every word of the conversation. The voice sounded young, so I didn't think the caller was the lady in the photo. But I was positive she could identify the woman. The caller wasn't threatening on the phone, more like evasive. Was she going to be a threat? Should I be worried about her? I looked at the screen and waited for her to call me back. It probably wouldn't be today, but I still sat and waited. Just in case.

***

Later that day I looked over the lunch menu, trying to avoid any conversation with the person opposite me. When Mum pulled up the driveway less than an hour ago, I didn't know what to do or how to react to her visit. Then she announced she was taking me out for lunch. That was the last thing I wanted to do with her. Small talk over salad? No thanks.

I knew she was watching, waiting for me to speak to her. Instead, I watched the pathway across the road along the Strand. It was busy now as holiday makers strolled along. There was a busker setting up his station for the day. He settled himself against the palm tree and adjusted his strings. The twang from the guitar echoed across the road.

'What are you having?' Mum asked.

I ignored her. The call this morning from my unidentified pen pal was enough of a shock. Then Mum arrived, unannounced. There was nothing to let me know she was coming. Only one brief call since she dumped me here and definitely no message about her visit today. Meanwhile, I was expected to drop everything and spend the rest of the day with her.

A waitress moved in our direction with a notepad and pen poised.

'I'll have the Caesar salad and a skinny cappuccino,' Mum ordered.

The waitress jotted it down and looked to me.

I passed her the menu. 'I'm not hungry, just an apple juice.'

'Shae,' said Mum, in her most restrained voice. 'You should eat some lunch.'

'Well, if I'd known we were having lunch I would have eaten a smaller breakfast.' I glared at her.

I actually only had a small bowl of cereal and I was hungry, but I didn't want to give Mum the satisfaction of doing a good gesture by taking me out for lunch.

'How are your holidays going?' She tried another attempt at conversation.

'Great.' Hopefully she picked up on the sarcasm.

'You're having fun?' she asked.

'What do you care?'

'Shae, please don't be cross with me.'

'It's a bit hard not to be. You said we were going to New Zealand together. That didn't happen. Instead, you ditched me for the summer holidays. Then you said you'd ring back the other night and that didn't happen either. Dad hasn't even rung me once. Where is he anyway?'

She swallowed hard then took a sip of water. 'Your father is a bit swamped at work.'

'Really? Because I thought he went away. Isn't that what you said? Besides, your work *always* closes over the Christmas break so what meeting did you have to go to?'

Mum watched me, her face tense. We were at a stalemate and I was not going to give an inch. She had to know I was suspicious of both of them. That I knew they were hiding something from me.

Mum's mobile rang. She snatched it up to check the caller ID. 'I've got to take this.'

I didn't understand why they wouldn't just tell me the truth about whatever was going on with them. The worst part was I didn't know who to be angrier at. Both had given me good reasons to be cross with them.

Chapter 14

I watched the boardwalk as I waited for Mum to take her call. There was a white bus with *Queensland Community Corrections* along the side blocking my view. Several people unloaded bicycles from the trailer at the rear. There was a group of people standing around clipping on helmets. A tall guy moved off to the side. He threw his head back to put a helmet on and my breath caught. I shrunk down and shoved a café menu in front of my face. If Callen looked my way there was nowhere for me to hide. But he didn't look, instead he fastened his helmet, collected one of the offloaded bicycles and joined the rest of the group. They finished getting ready and set off along the path that travelled around the foreshore. I watched until they were just a speck in the distance. Was *Community Corrections* some kind of volunteer thing? Is that what he meant by a lesson in life?

The chair in front of me scraped as Mum re-joined me. Soon after, the waitress appeared with our orders. I slurped my apple juice then pushed it away from me.

'Who was on the phone?' I asked.

She scrunched her hair and flicked it to the side. 'Actually, it was your father.'

'*What?*' I tried to reach for her phone but Mum jerked it away.

'You were speaking to Dad! Why didn't you let me talk to him?'

'Lower your voice please.' She kept her eyes down.

'Call him back and let me talk to him. Did he know you were with me?' I reached for her phone, but she snatched it from my reach.

'Shae, please. There are some things going on at the moment, but you don't need to know what they are just yet. We have them under control.'

'What does that mean?' I stood up.

She reached for me and grabbed my wrist. 'It means you need to trust me and not ask questions.'

'So, you admit that you're hiding something? Is that why you cancelled the New Zealand trip?'

Her face paled. She'd said too much.

'Please, Shae, just leave it alone.' Her voice broke. Her shoulders slouched, defeated.

This was a side of Mum I had not seen before. Maybe I had pushed her too far. I sighed loudly and plonked back on the seat, guilt bubbling to the surface. Why was I feeling guilty? I hadn't done anything wrong.

Mum pushed some of the lettuce around the plate not really eating anything. Her foundation did little to cover the dark circles beneath her eyes. I hadn't noticed them when she picked me up. Why didn't they just tell me what was going on? Mum looked up and caught me studying her.

I sighed and changed the topic. 'What does *Community Corrections* mean?' I indicated toward the bus across the road. 'A heap of people just got off and rode away on bikes.'

Mum followed my gaze. 'It's usually for people on a community service order. Offenders who have had their sentence suspended but still need to do something as punishment.'

'What kind of *offenders*?'

'Sometimes it's for people who can't pay their fines so they do community service to clear the debt. For others it might be a first-time offence. Community service means they are punished but escape jail as long as they keep out of trouble. Why?'

'No reason, just curious.' I slurped my empty juice glass.

Callen got off that bus, there was no mistaking that. There was also no other explanation for why he was on it. Mikayla's rumour about the bashing victim must be true.

Mum swallowed some more of her salad and wiped her mouth with the serviette. 'I'm just going to go to the toilet.'

Her phone buzzed not long after she left. I looked after Mum went but there was no sign of her. I debated Mum's need for privacy and my need to know more. Before I could stop myself. I grabbed her phone and opened the message. It was from Dad.

I will make this right again Susannah. I just need to know you're on my side. Are you?

I pictured Dad embracing the woman in the picture. They could be old friends and nothing more. But then who called me? Maybe the mystery caller was the woman in the picture after all. She could be young, like her voice. My stomach churned at the thought of my father with a younger woman. Maybe the caller hoped I would confront Dad and force him into admitting their affair.

I left the text message open for Mum to find and tried to put the pieces together. The answers I needed were not going to be found here. I had to go searching. Just as I made a decision, Mum appeared beside me. Her lips were pursed with hands gripped to the table. I followed her gaze. A dark green Commodore with tinted windows rolled past the cafe. A hand waved out the driver side window as they drove by. It was the third time I had seen that dint. Lexi's house, the shopping centre and now here. Somebody was following me, but why?

I slid the heavy green drapes across the lounge-room window, and closed and shut the front door. Today had been crazy. First Callen returned my missing necklace, then the mystery caller finally rang, then Mum's visit, and then discovering Callen was involved with *Community Corrections*. I was exhausted and just wanted to chill out with a movie.

'You two just sit there while I get everything organised.' I flicked off the lights and sank onto the couch.

Lexi grunted as I pushed her legs out of the way.

'Good to see you pulling your weight around here, Shayzie. Can't have you sponging off us all holidays,' teased Blake.

'Hey, how did lunch go with your mum today?' Lexi asked.

'It was … revealing.'

Blake scrunched up his face. 'How can a lunch be revealing?'

'Mind your business,' said Lexi. 'Now listen up Blakey boy. I was thinking we should have a pool party.' She changed the topic smoothly.

'Yeah, we definitely should!' said Blake, sitting up with excitement. 'You can invite the girls.'

'I think Dad's got a function coming up soon.' Lexi frowned. 'You have to ask them Blake, they trust you.'

'Of course they trust *me*. I don't sneak out my window to meet boys.'

'It wasn't to meet boys,' said Lexi. 'It was to meet Mikayla.'

'Yeah, who was meeting boys!' argued Blake.

Lexi threw a cushion at his head which he ducked easily. 'Just ask Dad about the party,' she said.

'Fine, but you'll owe me.'

'What for? It's going to be your party as much as mine,' Lexi argued.

'Maybe, but as you pointed out, they trust me. That means if you ask, they'll say no. But if I ask, they'll say yes. So, *you* will owe *me*.'

Blake leant back in the chair, satisfied with his logic. Lexi tossed another cushion. It knocked his cap sideways and wiped the smug look off his face.

'Oohh, we could invite Callen.' Lexi's eyes opened wide.

'Who is Callen?' asked Blake, shoving some popcorn in his mouth.

'The hottie from next door.' She smiled.

'How do you know his name's Callen? I thought it was Chris,' Blake said, grabbing more popcorn.

'Hey! Stop stuffing it in. The movie hasn't started yet.' Lexi snatched the bowl away.

'Lexi invited him over for a swim the other day,' I explained.

'Are you serious?' Blake looked interested now. 'So, did he bash that guy?'

'I didn't ask him to his face. I do have some tact. But Shae might know. She seems to know him better than me.'

Both cousins stared at me. The heat rose up my neck. 'I already explained how I spoke to him when I first got here.' I hadn't told Lexi that Callen helped me with my bike, or that he had found my necklace.

'And now you can explain what you know about him to me,' said Blake.

I couldn't help but smile at Blake playing the protective older cousin. At over six foot tall and solid as a rock, he was a bit intimidating in stature. But soft as a teddy bear in reality.

'There's nothing to explain! We had a small disagreement the day after I got here.'

'What do you mean disagreement?' Blake asked.

I shrugged. 'He nearly ran me over.'

'*What?*'

'Calm down, Blake. You'll pop a vein,' I joked. 'It was more like I ran into his car, but either way it was no big deal.'

'He calls her *Princess*,' said Lexi. 'I think he likes her.'

'Shut up!' I said throwing a cushion at her. 'He can't stand me more like it. Plus, this isn't about me. I didn't know he was the guy Lexi meant the other day and then she threw herself at him over the fence.'

'That part I can believe,' said Blake, slouching back against the furniture.

Lexi chucked the cushion at me this time, knocking me back against the couch.

'I didn't throw myself at him. I just wanted him to appreciate what's available.'

'I think he got the message loud and clear. *Oh Callen, look at my Cinderella locks. Oh Callen, look at my supermodel body*,' I teased.

I whacked her in the head with my pillow. We wrestled for control of it before spilling over the edge onto the ground.

'*Hey!*' Blake yelled. 'Can you two cut it out? The movie's about to start.'

I stood up. 'Anyone want a drink?'

Both of them mumbled yes.

'And more popcorn,' said Blake, passing me the bowl. 'I'll pause it after the intro.'

I walked toward the kitchen, passing my aunty and uncle's room along the way. Raised voices sounded from the other side of the door. I slowed down.

'She has a right to know,' said Uncle Kevin.

'Yes, she does!' said Aunty Liz. 'But do you want to be the one to tell her?'

'It's not right, Elizabeth. Shae is innocent in all this. Your sister needs to speak to her.'

Mum? What did Mum have to do with this? The picture was of Dad with another woman.

'Susannah might have done things differently, but it was Daniel's mess she cleaned up,' Aunty Liz's voice rose.

I shouldn't be listening, but I couldn't walk away. They knew something about the secret my parents were hiding. That much I was sure of.

'Shae's tougher than they think. She can handle this. It's not the worst news to get,' said Uncle Kevin.

'It's not the best news to hear either.'

It went silent on the other side of the door. I waited, but nothing else was said. Suddenly the door clicked open and Uncle Kevin emerged.

'Shae! You surprised me.'

'I was just getting some drinks before the movie started.' I forced a smile.

Aunty Liz joined us in the hallway.

'Well, I better get those drinks,' I said. 'Plus, Blake hogged all the popcorn.' It took all my strength not to turn back and ask what they were talking about.

By the time I got to the kitchen my hands were shaking. I looked through the window just as Callen walked across the lawn. He got inside the car and revved the engine. I waved through the lace curtain. The interior car light faded, but not before he waved back.

Chapter 15

I settled on the step near the front door with an oversized red apple. As I bit into it, juice spurted out and dripped down my finger. I wiped it against my denim shorts and took another bite, smaller this time. I shook out the bus timetable I had just printed off. There were only two buses a day between Townsville and Airlie Beach. They left in the morning and again in the afternoon. That worked perfectly in my favour. I could go home to have a look around, hopefully discover something that could explain all this mystery, then grab the next bus back. Nobody would know I'd even been back to Airlie Beach. I just hoped neither parent came home and caught me.

'Where are you sneaking off to?'

I jumped at Callen's voice. 'You should wear a bell to warn people instead of sneaking around, sheesh.'

He crossed his arms and leant against the house. I thought of him yesterday at the Strand with the *Queensland Community Corrections* bus parked on the street for all to see.

'That's one huge apple you've got there,' he said.

'Shut up, I'm hungry.'

'Don't let me stop you,' he laughed.

I took another bite, crunching in his direction.

'Callen,' Mr. Sampson called from his front door. 'Could you run down to the shops and get some milk please? We seem to have run out.'

'Sure, Pop.'

I waved at Mr. Sampson who returned the gesture. 'Your pop must like having you around.'

Callen shrugged. 'I guess. He gets lonely since Gran died a couple of years ago.'

'I'm sorry, I didn't know that.'

He shoved his hands in his pocket. 'It was a big shock. She wasn't sick a day in her life. Went swimming twice a week, volunteered at the bowls club and all that sort of stuff. She was full of energy.'

'How did she die?'

'A blood clot in her heart. She was asleep when it happened. Pop couldn't get her to wake up in the morning, but by then it was too late.'

A lump formed in my throat. I looked next door, but Mr. Sampson had already gone inside. What an awful tragedy for him. All my grandparents were still alive. I couldn't imagine something like that happening to them.

I took another bite and the crunch echoed in my ears. 'You must know a bit about bikes.'

I tried to keep the comment casual. If I was going to find out anything, Callen had to be the one to open up.

Callen tensed and straightened himself up. 'Why?'

'Well, you fixed the tube in my tyre.'

'Oh that.' He shrugged. 'It wasn't too hard to work out.'

Maybe I was being too subtle. Time to step it up a gear. Would he come clean about the *Community Corrections*?

I reached for my stone and dragged it along the chain. 'Actually, I saw you yesterday.'

His eyebrows pulled together before the realization of where I must have seen him flashed across his face. 'What did you see?'

'You, obviously. And a heap of other riders along the Strand.' I deliberately didn't mention the bus. If he wanted to tell me about it then this was his chance. The silence stretched out between us. I held my breath waiting for his response.

'It was a good day for a bike ride.' He dropped his gaze.

Disappointment flooded through me. The opportunity for Callen to confide in me couldn't have been more obvious. Damn it! Maybe he was testing me to see how much I know, or maybe he didn't trust me. Either way, his omission was as good as a lie.

'What were you doing at the Strand?' he asked.

'My mum was in town and took me out for lunch.'

'That must have been nice.'

I scrunched up my nose. 'Not really.' This time it was me who dropped their gaze. Thankfully Callen didn't push it any further.

Instead, he snatched the map from my hand. 'Where are you off to anyway?'

'Hey! Give it back.' I stood up and tried to grab it, but he was taller and held it higher than I could reach.

He squinted to read the destination. 'Airlie Beach? Aren't Townsville beaches good enough for you?' He lowered the timetable to my level.

I grabbed the timetable back from him. 'Mind your business.'

I bit my apple and folded the map back up. I didn't want anyone to know where I was going. I wasn't even going to tell Lexi. At least not unless I found out something about this whole mess.

'If you really want to go there, I could give you a lift,' Callen suggested.

'Why would you do that?' More importantly could I trust him not to tell anybody.

'Well, I've hardly left Pop's place since I got here. It could be fun.'

Callen crossed his arms and rolled back and forth on his feet.

Was he daring me to refuse his offer?

'You know it's a three-hour drive, right? One way.'

He shrugged. 'I don't mind.'

I shook my head. 'I don't think so.'

'Come on, I need a change of scenery. Pop's great, but I have to get away. There are only so many games of cards I can play.'

'Thanks for the offer, but you don't have to do that,' I said

'Shae, please. Just let me drive you.' His brooding dark eyes fixed on me.

I wavered from their effect and found myself nodding. 'Okay.'

'Great, it's a date.' He smiled.

'No, it's not.'

Callen laughed. '7am. Be ready.'

He turned to leave then stopped. 'What's so urgent in Airlie Beach anyway?'

I swallowed. 'Guess we'll find out when we get there.' Trust and honesty worked both ways. If he didn't want to share all the details about life, then neither did I.

His eyes narrowed, but he didn't ask any more questions. I went inside, closing the front door behind me.

'Who were you talking to?' Blake asked, repositioning himself on the couch.

'When?'

'Just now. I heard you talking to somebody. You didn't sign us up for pay TV by any chance, did you?' he asked.

I shook my head.

'Too bad. I've been trying to talk the folks into getting it, but they won't listen.'

I tried to walk off.

'So, who were you talking to?' Blake persisted.

'It was Callen from next door.'

Blake sat up. 'Really? Why was he sniffing around?'

'Relax, he fixed my bike the other day and I was just talking to him about that.'

It wasn't a complete lie. We did talk about bikes.

'Fine. But I'll be watching, Shayzie!' He pointed his finger at me.

I continued down the hall to Lexi's room and found her sprawled on the bed. She pulled the ear-pieces out when I entered. When we were younger, I always slept in Lexi's room on the trundle bed. We still did that occasionally, but with Aileen living overseas I got my own bedroom when I stayed now.

'Lexi, I need a huge favour, but you're not allowed to ask any questions.' The words spilled out fast.

I waited for the barrage of questions, but she controlled her impulse to know everything. Instead, she patted the bed cover beside her. 'I'm listening.'

I closed her door. 'I need you to cover for me tomorrow because I might be late for tea.'

'Why would you be late?' she asked.

'No questions, remember?'

She opened her mouth, then promptly closed it. Her brain must have been in overdrive, but she managed to show more restraint than I thought possible.

'I promise I'll fill you in, but for the moment I just need you to agree to this, okay?'

She didn't say anything.

'Lexi?'

'You said don't talk.'

'I said no questions, you can still talk,' I said.

'Fine, I'll cover for you, but I want *all* the details when you get home.'

I squeezed her with a hug. 'Thanks, you're the best!'

'Shae, there will be questions!'

I didn't want to think about what *all* the details might be. I hoped there were some answers waiting for me at home, but my immediate problem was the car ride. It would be hot, sweaty and confined. There would be nowhere to hide from Callen. He better have air conditioning.

Chapter 16

The next morning, we set off early as arranged. After some brief but polite conversation we settled into a comfortable ride. Music played quietly as we drove along the highway. I tried to stop my foot from tapping as the outside world passed me by. This was a big gamble to take by going home. What if my parents caught me? How would I explain my trip back home? I had to make sure not to get caught. I also had to make sure I found something that would help explain this weird situation. There had to be something at home.

A service station loomed in the distance and Callen indicated to turn in.

'I need some petrol,' he explained.

'That's okay, I'll use the toilet,' I said.

I didn't really need to pee, but I couldn't think of another way to pay for the fuel. I knew he wouldn't let me give him any cash. That would only embarrass him.

Callen got out to fill the car up while I went inside to wait near the counter and pay. As soon as he started to make his way inside, I handed over my bank card to the attendant.

I met Callen as the automatic doors slid open.

'It's all done,' I said, trying to walk past him before he could object.

'What do you mean?'

'The petrol, it's been paid,' I said, without slowing down.

Callen followed behind me then climbed in the driver seat.

'Shae, that wasn't the deal,' he said.

'It was, I just hadn't told you yet.' I held his stare and shrugged. 'It's no big deal. You're the one doing me the favour.'

He nodded once and started the engine. I looked out the window and released the breath I had been holding.

***

'Do not park out the front,' I instructed as he pulled alongside the concrete curb. 'Keep going.'

He continued further down the street, then turned the engine off. 'Is this good enough?'

'Perfect.' I looked about the street but it was empty at this time of day. Most of the neighbours would be at work so there should be nobody to spot me and report back to my parents. I climbed out of the car and strode toward my house.

We walked up the path in the middle of the manicured lawn. It was surrounded by matching bushes of orange and purple flowers. A landscaper designed it with lots of earthy tones to frame the spongy green grass. We arrived at the frosted glass door to my home. Callen emitted a low whistle as he walked inside. 'So, this is where you live.'

'Was it the poster sized family portrait that gave it away?'

I hated that thing hanging there. It was the first thing anyone saw when they came inside. It was embarrassing!

Callen walked into the first room on the right. 'Woah, check out the size of your TV!'

'We only really watch movies on that one.'

I tried to see things as if it were the first time, like Callen. I found myself embarrassed by the exorbitance. The theatre room as Dad called it, was hardly ever used. DVDs were lined up in rows along floating shelves. There must have been at least two hundred in the collection. Dad prided himself on being 'old school' and still watching DVDs. The plush leather couch had a reclining chair at each end. The speakers provided a surround sound system to rival any movie theatre. Everything was state of the art. Dad was a bit of a movie buff when he had time. Callen settled into the recliner and pushed it back. His legs flicked out from beneath him. 'Where's the popcorn?'

'Do you want a choc top ice-cream as well?' I asked, amused.

He laughed and put the footrest back into place. I looked around, but it all looked the same as before I left. Down the hallway to the right was the double door entryway to my parents' room. I cringed because I knew what Callen was going to find in there.

'This must be the *master* room.'

He strolled past me and spun around taking in everything at once. The whole space was double the size of a normal room. It included a parent's retreat, a trendy addition they chose to include. I'm not sure what my parents needed to retreat from. There were only three of us living here.

A giant plasma television was set up on the wall, directly across from the king size bed. In the corner was another couch with a coffee table in front. A discarded book lay face down.

'This is insane!' Callen called out from behind the false wall.

I followed his voice knowing he had found enough items to clothe a small village. There was even an electric rotating shoe holder for my parents' footwear. Their clothes were hung according to colour, compliments of the interior designer Mum hired.

'My mum likes to shop,' I said, as if to explain the over-the-top wardrobe.

Callen moved down a short passage toward the ensuite. Dark speckled tiles covered every surface from the double shower to the twin basins and all over the surrounding walls. He looked at me with one eyebrow raised and gestured toward the floating toilet. I raised the lid and closed it again. A quiet flush followed.

'Does a brush pop out to clean your bum as well?' Callen asked.

'Why don't you use it and find out?' I suggested.

I dragged him from the opulence of my parents' domain toward the kitchen. The sight stopped me in my tracks. A pile of unpaid bills sat on the counter, pizza boxes and take away containers were discarded near the stove, while dishes were stacked in the sink. I reached over and pulled the stool out to sit on before my legs gave way.

'Is today the maid's day off?' Callen teased.

I shook my head. 'We don't have a maid.'

'I was joking.'

Somehow, I didn't think he was joking. We had a house cleaner, although I wasn't going to admit that to Callen. He probably already thought we were overindulged snobs. But when I looked at him, his face was laced with sympathy, not judgment.

'Shae, why are we here?'

Good question. What did I hope to achieve by coming back here? Did I really think the answers would be lying around here somewhere? If my parents hadn't clued me in with what was happening yet, they definitely wouldn't leave anything incriminating out in the open to be found easily.

I took a deep breath. 'We were supposed to go on a family holiday this summer, except my parents cancelled it at the last minute. No explanation, no warning. They just cancelled it and said I had to stay with my cousins. I love staying with Blake and Lexi. Dale and Aileen are great as well, but they're both older and have moved out so I don't see them as much anymore.

'Then the other night I overheard my aunty and uncle talking about how I had a right to know about what was going on. Plus, my dad hasn't spoken to me since they dropped me off. He always rings me, no matter what.' I could tell Callen wasn't convinced there was a problem.

'Let me get this right. You're on your own for the holidays AND your folks don't call to check in. Based on that you think there's a conspiracy theory going on?'

'Something like that.' I knew how it sounded, but I also knew about the picture.

'Well, it sounds like a sweet deal to me. Maybe you're overreacting a bit?'

When he explained it like that, it did sound kind of stupid. But I hadn't told him everything. I wanted to tell him about the photo, but I couldn't. That was too personal to share when I didn't know what it meant. I was ignoring the obvious meaning because I couldn't think about Dad having an affair.

I rifled through some of the papers scattered across the bench in front of me but found nothing of interest. Then I remembered the safe in the pool house. That would make a great hiding spot!

'Follow me,' I said.

The back door slammed behind me as I ran outside. I lifted the safety lock on the pool gate and walked into the bar area.

'This place just keeps getting better and better!' said Callen.

I ignored him while he checked out the well-stocked bar. Instead, I squatted down behind the bar and slid the cupboard across. The fingerprint activated safe was hidden inside. Only three people could access it. Dad, Mum and me. Dad made it that way in case something ever happened to them. The thing was bolted to the ground so there was no chance of it getting stolen. I had never opened it except for that one time to check our fingerprints worked. I pressed my thumb against the sensor and waited. The red-light changed to green and the door clicked ajar. Callen bent down beside me. My mind tried to catch up with the sight before me.

'Whoah! Hasn't your family heard of a bank?'

I pulled out the neatly stacked piles of cash. 'How much do you think is there?'

An elastic band secured fifty-dollar notes into half a dozen bundles. I passed them to Callen who lined them up on the bar. A mobile phone was hidden behind the cash. I pressed the *on* button. Nothing happened. I tried again but got the same result.

'Must be flat,' he said, sitting it next to the money.

I looked inside the safe again. There were some manila folders with documents inside. I flicked through them but found nothing of interest. Birth certificates, passports, marriage certificate and university degrees. There were a couple of invoices for services to Lang, Lang & Co. solicitors, but I couldn't tell what the services had been. There was nothing else inside the safe that screamed conspiracy.

I stood up and took in the impressive sight of notes before me. My family was wealthy, but my parents didn't make a habit of leaving piles of cash lying around the place.

'There must be over thirty grand here,' Callen said. 'Who did you say your parents were? Drug dealers?'

'Ha, ha. *Not* funny.'

All that exposed money was making me nervous. I worked hard to keep my fingers steady as I returned the cash to the safe. I tried to stack it the way it had been found.

'What about this?' Callen dangled the mobile phone in front of my face.

I took it. 'There has to be a charger somewhere inside.' I slammed the safe shut and waited for the red light to flash before replacing the fake wall.

I took a breath and tried to process what I just found. 'That was a lot of money,' I said.

'Sure you didn't want to take a pile? We could have had a lot of fun with it.'

I ignored him and went back to the house. The phone was hidden in the safe with all that money for a reason. I needed a charger to find out what was on that phone. One thing our house had was plenty of gadgets.

Chapter 17

In my parents' bedroom there were chargers on either side of the bed, but neither fit. I collided with Callen on the way back out.

'Hey, slow down.'

But I couldn't slow down. I couldn't stop until I knew more. If the phone would just turn on, I knew it would tell me something important. I moved down the hallway toward the study, but something stopped me as I neared my room. The double bed was still made and undisturbed. The colourful marble ink doona cover was a huge contrast to the white walls and the rest of the furniture in my room. My iPad sat on the bedside table with slippers abandoned beneath the bed. Nothing had changed, yet everything was different.

'So, this is your room.'

I jumped at the closeness of Callen's voice. Warmth from his body reached mine, not touching, yet they might as well be.

'You could invite me in if you want,'

'As if I would want to do that.' I elbowed him in the stomach, even though my body was doing weird things.

'Oww.' He doubled over, staggered across the threshold to my room and collapsed on my bed. 'I think you broke a rib.'

'No, I didn't.' I crossed my arms and leant against the doorway.

Callen stretched out and tucked his hands behind his head.

'Comfortable? Would you like a teddy bear or something?' I asked.

'I bet you used to have dolls on your bed. Lots of dolls,' he teased.

'Why? Because I'm such a princess?'

'You are definitely a princess, but maybe not the kind I first thought.'

I didn't know how to interpret his comment. He sat up, watching me. My mouth became dry. I couldn't look at him, yet I couldn't turn away.

He swung his legs over the edge. 'What's going on here, Shae?'

I didn't know if he was talking about my parents or us, so I answered honestly to both. 'I have no idea.'

His hand reached out for me from the bed. Was he offering me friendship, or more? I didn't wait to find out and turned away. *Focus, Shae!* Callen was not allowed to distract me. I left him sitting on my bed and didn't look back. At the end of the house, I flung the study door open.

'Woah!' I stopped still.

The filing cabinet doors were ajar, like a set of steps. Piles of folders were scattered all about. I tiptoed through the cardboard mess, careful not to stand on anything and slumped on the chair.

Callen appeared, but he paused in the doorway. 'Looks like someone was trying to find something.'

'This doesn't make sense. None of this is normal,' I said, frustrated with still having no answers.

'You don't have to figure it all out today,' Callen said.

'I have to try.' I rifled through the desk drawers. 'Gotcha!'

I shoved the charger in the wall and plugged in the phone. The red charge symbol flashed. I tugged against my necklace as the phone powered up.

'Just do it,' said Callen. 'Turn it on.'

I held my breath and pressed the button. It vibrated as it came to life and I tapped the messages icon. There was only one stream of conversation.

> *9:15, 31 Oct*
> I need to see you.

> *22:17, 31 Oct*
> I will ring you from work. Do not ring me Karen.

> *20:30, 1 Nov*
> Can we meet Wednesday at Horseshoe Bay Cafe in Bowen? 12pm.

> *6:29, 2 Nov*
> Yes. Susannah still doesn't know so be discreet.

> *21:23, 10 Nov*
> You can't just ignore this.

> *8:05, 11 Nov*
> I'm not! I have family obligations and you've turned everything upside down.

> *13:47, 2 Dec*
> Either you tell her or I will. I didn't want it to be this way Daniel.

> *21:11, 2 Dec*
> I'm begging you not to tell her. It will devastate her.

I blinked back tears and clenched my shaking hands. In an instant Callen covered them with his. He squeezed my hands and I didn't pull away. 'It's okay. We'll work this out together,' he said.

I passed him the phone. 'Read it. I think I've already figured it out.'

Callen scrolled through the messages. 'Susannah's your mum?'

I nodded, unable to speak. My stomach twisted and I thought I might throw up. Breathe in. Breathe out. Deep breath in. Deep breath out.

'Are you okay? You've gone really pale.' he said.

'Just give me a minute. It will pass.'

Callen waited patiently while I desperately tried to settle my gut. After a while I nodded. 'I'm okay now. Sorry about that.'

Callen didn't look convinced, but he didn't push it any further. I read the messages once more. This time I copied them down, along with the dates.

'Do you think she knows about the affair?' asked Callen.

'Why do you think it's an affair?' I desperately wanted to believe the message. *It's not what you think.*

'Shae, it's kind of obvious.'

'Shut up!' I stood up. 'You don't know anything about it.'

I pushed past him and stormed out. I knew Callen was right and he hadn't even seen the picture. Put the two things together and it was kind of obvious. So, what was actually going on? Was Dad trying to bribe this woman to stay quiet? Is that what all the money was for, or was she bribing him? Footsteps stopped next to me.

'I'm sorry,' I said, without looking at him. 'It wasn't fair to take this mess out on you.'

'It's fine, I get it. Trust me, I understand deception.'

I turned toward him. 'I still shouldn't have yelled at you.'

He stepped closer. 'Shae, it's okay.'

I was level with his nose. His hand gripped my chin lightly, tipping it upwards. His mouth moved toward mine. Was this happening? Did I want this? Suddenly the side fence squeaked open. Callen pulled me down as a figure passed by the window. The footsteps faded as they walked toward the pool house.

I tried to stand, but Callen held me tight. 'Just wait a minute,' he said.

I shrugged him off. 'Let me up.'

He released his grip and I peeked out the window. A man with white hair paused at the safety gate. There was something familiar about him.

'I take it that's not your dad?' Callen asked.

'Nope. Not unless he's aged 20 years.'

We stood silently and waited. The clock tick, tick, ticked through the silence.

A recent memory came to mind. I was squatting in the garage adjusting the bike chain when I heard raised voices. One was Dad's, but I didn't know the other.

'You don't owe her anything,' the man insisted.

'Maybe not, but it's the right thing to do,' said dad.

'What does Susannah think?' the man asked.

'I haven't told her yet.'

'She needs to know. You have to tell her.'

'I will, but first just find out what I need to know and then I'll tell Susannah. Damn it, John! I can't believe this is happening. I won't let it ruin my family.'

Dad's voice had drifted off as he passed the garage window and the man followed. I gasped as I realized it was the same man outside right now!

'What?' Callen asked.

The pool gate creaked and the man emerged. Callen didn't need to drag me down a second time. The footsteps grew closer, louder. They paused at the kitchen window then moved off. The side gate slammed closed and I ran down toward the theatre room. I had to see him again. A shadow near the front window spooked me and I jerked back smacking into Callen. He groaned.

'You're bleeding.' I looked back and forth between him and the front window.

'I'm fine. Go!' he said.

A car engine started as I leapt onto the couch. A dark green Commodore with tinted windows pulled out from the curb. The rear end was dinted.

Chapter 18

The drive back to Townsville was subdued. Callen dropped me off without any questions. He seemed good at knowing when to push and knowing when to back off.

'Thanks for the lift,' I said. 'And sorry about your nose.'

He wiggled it. 'I'll live.'

I waved goodbye and ran up the porch steps.

Inside I barged into Lexi's room. 'Where's your computer?'

'Hello cousin whose been gone all day!' she replied.

'*Lexi*!'

'Have a rough day?'

I sighed. 'I'm sorry but please, Lexi, I really need your computer.'

'Where's yours? Doesn't everyone at your school have one?'

I pictured the iPad on my bedside table, which made me think of Callen lying on my bed. I shook the image from my head. 'Can I just use the stupid laptop? I've got an idea.'

She shoved her laptop across the bed and sat at her desk. 'What's the rush? Got a hot date online?' Lexi brushed her hair as she watched me in the reflection of her mirror.

I wanted to share my suspicions with her, if only to ease the weight of them bearing down on me. After the way she had acted lately, I didn't know if I could.

'Lexi, can I trust you?'

'What kind of question is that? It should be *me* asking you that.'

'Why?'

'I know whose car you just got out of.' She smirked. 'You have a bit of explaining to do, Shayzie.'

I felt the blush in my cheeks at being caught out. 'I will tell you everything.' I couldn't really deny it, could I? 'But please don't ask me about Callen this second.'

'Shae, what the hell is going on with you?'

'Promise not to say a word to anyone? Not even Blake.' I slumped on her bed.

'You're really starting to freak me out,' she said.

'You remember that photo of Dad? Well, I went home today,' I explained.

'What? You went all the way to Airlie Beach. Did you go with Callen?'

'Lexi, focus. I went home and found a mobile phone with messages to someone called *Karen*. I think it's the woman in the picture. I think she's been seeing my dad.'

Lexi shook her head. 'I can't believe you went home to Airlie Beach.'

'Really? That's all you can say about the whole story.' I huffed and turned my back on her.

'Oh, come on, Shae! A road trip home, a secret mobile, an affair?'

'Who said it was an affair? Why do people keep jumping to that conclusion?' My eyes welled and I squeezed back the tears.

After a moment, Lexi squeezed my shoulder.

I grabbed her hand. 'I'm sorry.'

'Me too. What can I do?'

'Come closer, I have a hunch about something.' I turned on the computer while Lexi peered over my shoulder. 'I think Karen's the one who sent the picture to force Dad to come clean. I think she's blackmailing him.' I brought up Mum's email address, followed by the password I created: *Shaerulz*.

Lexi swatted my arm. 'You're hacking your mother's email?'

'It's not hacking when you already know the details.'

Lexi's mouth formed a round shape. 'You naughty thing. Who are you and what have you done with my cousin?'

I poked my tongue out and scrolled through the emails looking for female names. There was a lot of junk to navigate through. I clicked on Sarah Turrow. No good. There was another one from Claire Hangly. It was just a thank you from a satisfied client. I scrolled to November. There was an email from somebody called John Lang. That name was familiar so I clicked on it.

'Aha!' I said, getting excited by the discovery.

Dear Susannah,

I will look into the matter we discussed. I want to convey that I have reservations about doing this. I have a colleague who is more familiar with family law than I am. I will reach out to her. I will be in touch once I have something more for you.

Regards,
John Lang.

The signature was Lang, Lang & Co solicitors.

'What does that mean?' Lexi asked.

'I don't know, but there were invoices from this firm in the safe at home.'

'What were the invoices for?'

'I didn't read them,' I groaned.

'Don't worry, keep looking. Maybe try the deleted messages folder?' suggested Lexi.

'Good idea.' I clicked on the deleted button and scrolled through.

A name appeared several times. *Karen Fields.* I clicked on the most recent. The conversation dated back nearly two months. I scrolled down to read upwards.

Subject: Clock's ticking
Date: Fri, 15 Nov, 2021 6:40; 01 +1030

Susannah,

There's something you need to know. I'm sorry, but what's done is done.

Karen

Subject: RE; Clock's ticking
Date: Wed, 20 Nov, 2021 1:39; 01 +1030

Karen,

Do you have any idea what this means?

Susannah

Subject: RE; Clock's ticking
Date: Fri, 21 Nov, 2021 11:41; 01 +1030

Don't forget that you are part of this Susannah. This isn't just Daniel's mistake.

Karen

Subject: RE; Clock's ticking
Date: Wed, 22 Nov, 2021 1:39; 01 +1030

How could I forget? I blame myself as much as Daniel. Just give me more time.

Susannah

Subject: RE; Clock's ticking
Date: Fri, 3 Dec, 2021 13:41; 01 +1030

I'm sorry but time is up. You need to do something or I will.

Karen

Subject: RE; Clock's ticking
Date: Sat, 4 Dec, 2021 7:35; 01 +1030

Just let us get through Christmas at least. Please.

Susannah

I realised I'd been holding my breath and pushed it out. 'There can't be two Karens'.'

The text and emails had to be from the same person, but it didn't make any sense. I pulled out the piece of paper scribbled with the dates and text messages from the phone. I double checked the dates.

'No way! There has to be a mistake.' I cross checked the dates again and there was no denying it.

'She knew!' I looked at Lexi with fear. 'Mum's known all along.'

Did Dad have any idea that Mum knew? If he did, why was Karen telling Dad to tell her?

I rubbed at my temples. This revelation was bigger than I expected. What was I going to do with this new information?

'Let me get this right,' said Lexi. 'This chick, Karen, was demanding your dad confess except your mum already knew, and then someone sent you a picture.'

'And called me. The other day a girl called asking if I got her letter.'

'Was it this woman Karen?'

I shrugged. 'She wouldn't tell me anything. Just said we had to meet and she'd ring me.'

'Shae, why did you say blackmail before?' asked Lexi.

'There were piles of cash in the safe at home. I think it's for Karen to shut her up.'

Lexi shook her head. 'This is just like a movie, Shae, and you're in way over your head.'

I groaned and lay back on the bed. There was so much more happening here. It couldn't just be an affair. Secret phone, secret texts, secret piles of money. There were too many secrets. But who was keeping the biggest one of all? Karen or my parents?

Chapter 19

'Are you sure I can come and watch?' I asked.

'Yeah, of course,' said Lexi.

'Promise not to make me join in?' I crossed my arms.

'Shae, they're little kids. How bad can you be compared with them?'

'Have you forgotten the dance routines we used to do in front of everyone?' I reminded her.

'We were eight! You must have gotten better since then and if not, then you can pretend!'

We hurried toward the dance studio. Lexi ran school holiday dance classes for little kids. She taught them simple routines and tried to encourage them to join the club afterwards.

Wham! Out of nowhere I collided with a man in a suit. He turned to apologise.

'Dad!'

'Shae?'

'What are you doing here?' I demanded. We were outside the Townsville University Hospital. 'Were you just in there?'

He shook his head. 'I mean yes, I was in there but uhmm, not for me. I'm not sick. I was visiting … uhmm … I was seeing a client.'

Lexi checked her watch. 'Hi Uncle Daniel. Sorry to break up

your reunion, but we have to go, Shae, or I'll be late.'

I ignored her. 'You *were* going to visit me, weren't you?'

'Of course! I was going to surprise you,' he answered.

My shoulders remained stiff, unconvinced.

Dad ruffled my hair. 'Now you've spoilt the surprise.'

'Don't worry, I'm still very much surprised,' I said.

Dad's eyes flitted around before his face relaxed. 'I'm sorry sweetheart, but my ride is here and I have a meeting to get to. I'll see you tonight at Lexi's.'

Dad opened the door of the waiting car. The man I saw back home in Airlie Beach sat in the driver seat.

'*Dad!*'

'What's wrong, Shae?'

I waved him toward me. 'Who's that man in the car?'

'John? He's our lawyer, why?'

'Does your lawyer always drive you around?' I asked.

'He gets paid good money to do a lot of things, Shae.'

Lexi grabbed my arm. 'Come on Shae! We gotta go.'

She dragged me down the street. I turned back and watched the car drive away. The dint in the rear was unmistakable.

'Okay, spill. What was that all about?' said Lexi.

'That guy, John the lawyer, he was at my house the day I went home.'

'Did he see you there?' she asked.

'No, I was too busy hiding under the bench while he snooped around the pool house.'

'Well, he works for your dad. He was probably getting something for him.'

My eyebrows raised. 'From the pool house?'

Lexi shrugged. 'I don't know, but I do know we're late. Run!'

We arrived in time and spent the next 90 minutes choreographing dance steps for fourteen little girls and two boys. Lexi even gave me a group to look after. The parents should have got a refund for my pathetic efforts, but the kids didn't seem to mind.

'Do not *ever* make me do that again,' I said as we waited on the curb for our lift.

Lexi nudged me. 'You did great.'

'Oh yeah, *Australia's Got Talent* here I come.'

Honk, honk! Kai's car rumbled in front of us and we scrambled inside.

'Thank goodness that's over,' Lexi huffed.

Kai curled his arm around her neck. He pulled her toward him and kissed her briefly. 'Better now?'

'A little bit.' She kissed Kai back and he moved in for a longer pash.

Simon groaned. 'You two make me sick.'

'You're just jealous, mate,' said Kai.

'Of what? Turning into a marshmallow?'

Kai looked at me. 'Of not having someone who appreciates you.'

Simon ignored the comment. 'I have my teddy bear at home. Coco does a great job of keeping me company.'

Kai started the car. 'I have to pick up my sister and drop her somewhere. It won't take long.'

'Sondra?' said Lexi. 'Do you mean I'll finally get to meet her?'

She looked at me wide-eyed. I knew exactly what she was thinking, but there was no way she could bring up Callen with Kai in the car.

As we drove along Simon leant toward me. 'Did you shake your groove thing with Lexi?'

'Humph, hardly.'

'Shae is as coordinated at dancing as she is at roller-skating,' said Lexi.

'How bad are you?' Simon asked.

'You'll see tonight at the disco,' I said.

'Shae once managed to break her arm just by standing still on the four wheels,' said Lexi.

Simon laughed. 'Seriously? How?'

I shrugged. 'I wasn't even moving and down I went.'

'Remember Blake ran home to tell Mum? But she wasn't there because Dale had already called her.'

Kai turned into a driveway where double gates greeted us with a touch pad to open them.

'You weren't kidding,' I whispered to Simon.

Kai punched in some numbers and drove up the circular driveway. He honked the horn and instantly a slim girl with short, dark hair appeared.

She skipped down the steps and opened my door. 'Oops, I didn't know the car was full.'

'We'll fit,' I said, sliding across to the middle.

Simon moved over to make some room. It was a squash with the three of us in the back seat.

Kai pointed at Lexi and me as he introduced us. 'You already know Simon,' he added.

'Hi,' Sondra said, quietly.

Kai skidded as he drove off.

'I wouldn't do that, Dad's inside.'

'What's he gonna do?' Kai said, but eased off the accelerator.

Lexi fiddled with the radio then turned to face Sondra. 'It's nice to finally meet you.'

Sondra smiled. 'I know right? I've been nagging Kai to introduce us.'

'You go to St. Pat's, don't you? What's it like with no boys?'

Trust Lexi to ask that question.

Sondra shrugged. 'It's no big deal. I don't know any different, so I can't really compare.'

'Is Mum picking you up?' Kai asked.

'Yeah, you don't have to,' she answered.

Lexi looked out the window. 'Hey, can you pull in and grab me a drink?'

'What?' said Kai.

'After all that dancing I need a drink, *pleeaase*.'

Kai grunted but turned into the service station.

'Just a bottle of water,' she called after him.

My body tensed as my sneaky cousin turned to Sondra. 'Is it true you went out with a guy called Callen?'

Sondra pushed her hair behind her ears. 'Uhh, yeah.'

'How long?'

'Long enough to know it was the biggest mistake of my life,' she answered.

I forced my head not to move and my mouth to stay shut.

'Are the rumours true?' asked Lexi.

Sondra shifted in the seat. 'Do you know him?'

'Sort of. He's staying next door,' said Lexi.

'Then you can ask him yourself.'

'Sorry, I'm being rude,' said Lexi, trying to backtrack. 'You don't have to answer, it's just that he *is* staying next door so I wondered about him.'

'You want some advice?' Her tone was vicious. 'Don't believe a word that comes out of that lying snake's mouth.'

Chapter 20

Later that night before we sat down for tea, Lexi pulled me aside. 'Are you going to ask your dad tonight?'

'What exactly should I ask him?'

'Show him the photo and ask him straight out,' she said.

'I can't do that.'

'Why not? There's a reason we ran into him today. He's here now, so ask him. Don't waste this chance.'

I tugged on my necklace. 'Do you think he was really going to come see me today? I mean if I hadn't run into him.'

Lexi shook her head.

'Me neither.'

'Girls! Tea's ready,' Aunty Liz called out.

Dad patted the chair beside him. I forced a smile and sat down.

'Are you sure you don't want to spend the night? You should have told us you were coming, Daniel.' Aunty Liz said. 'We would have put on a better dinner than tacos.'

'It's okay, Liz. It was a last-minute trip and work foots the bill for the motel so it's fine. Besides, I love tacos. It's one thing Susannah can cook.'

Laughter spread around the table. We had all been victims of Mum's cooking skills.

'So, how was the dance class, Lexi? I bet Shae was a great help,' said Dad.

'She was very helpful,' said Lexi, piling on the lettuce. 'She helped a girl called Karen.'

I glared at Lexi, but it didn't stop her. '*Karen* needs a bit of help sometimes. She's not very good at following instructions.'

Dad ruffled my hair. 'There might be a dance teacher hiding in you after all.'

'I doubt it,' I said

The phone trilled in the background.

'I'll get it,' said Uncle Kevin, jumping up. 'Aileen, how are you?' Uncle Kevin gestured for my aunt to join him.

She dropped her half-eaten taco and almost ripped the phone from his ear. 'Aileen? It's Mum, how are you sweetheart? How's ... everything going?' She walked out of the room.

Lexi raised an eyebrow at Blake who shrugged and kept eating.

Uncle Kevin coughed. 'Aileen uhh, wasn't feeling great the last time they spoke.'

'Why, what's wrong with her?' asked Lexi.

'Aww you know, just stuff. Your mother can tell you.' He looked at my dad a moment too long.

'Was it serious or just a bug?' asked Lexi.

'Your mum will explain when she comes back.'

With perfect timing Aunty Liz walked back into the kitchen.

'Is Aileen feeling better?' Lexi said. 'Oohh, maybe her pommie boyfriend knocked her up and she's got morning sickness.'

'Yeah right,' said Blake.

He threw a wedge of tomato that splatted on her plate and she shrieked.

'Cut it out!' Uncle Kevin pushed his chair back.

I looked up, shocked. Uncle Kevin never yelled.

'I was only joking,' said Lexi. 'As if Aileen would get pregnant. Her life is completely planned out.'

'*Lexi*. Stop. Talking.' Uncle Kevin rubbed his face, but a serious expression remained.

Aunty Liz cleared her throat. 'Aileen has some news she wanted me to share with you.'

The pause was long.

'No way! Is Lexi, right?' Blake asked.

I waited for my aunty to deny it, but she didn't. 'Aileen and Christian … are having a baby.'

'They've been together like, five minutes,' said Lexi.

'Five months actually, but it doesn't matter. It might not have been planned, but they are committed to each other. They've chosen to have this child and we will support them.' Aunty Liz rushed from the kitchen and Uncle Kevin followed after her.

'Holy shit, did that just happen?' said Blake.

My cousins stared at their plates. Dad gave me a weak smile.

'Did you know?' I asked him.

He nodded. 'It wasn't my place to say anything. They wanted to wait until Aileen had been to a doctor to confirm it.'

Aileen, the straight A student who always had her nose in a book and had never been grounded a day in her life. Aileen, the only cousin who missed parties to stay home on weekends and study. Aileen, who had never participated in anything spontaneous in her life, was pregnant.

How many other secrets were being kept in this family?

We finished dinner with the crunch of taco shells the only sound in the room.

***

'Sorry I can't stay, but I've got paperwork to catch up on,' said Dad as I walked him outside.

I shrugged. 'It's fine. We're going to this roller-skating thing anyway.'

'I'll call you tomorrow night.' He opened his car door.

'*Dad.*' This was my last chance to say something.

'What is it, Shae?'

I rushed across to him. I opened my mouth except no words came out. The printed image was burning a hole in my pocket. I just couldn't believe that Dad would be having an affair. He was not that kind of person. He was hard working and reliable and he loved us, especially Mum. I'd heard how they fell in love a hundred times.

'She didn't want anything to do with me at first, Shayzie, but she soon fell for my charms. It took a cappuccino every day for a week before she gave in and agreed to dinner. One dinner, that's all it took. I knew I had to impress her so we went to an expensive restaurant that I couldn't afford back then. Well, the portions were so small that we were still hungry afterwards. So, we picked up pizza and went back to her house. I knew after three slices I was going to marry her.'

'Shae, I have to go.' Dad interrupted my thoughts.

I tried again, but no words formed.

Dad sighed. 'I know you're still upset about the cancelled trip.' He reached out to squeeze my shoulder. 'I promise it will only be a little longer and you'll be home.'

'Will you be there?' I asked.

'Of course, why wouldn't I?'

'I don't know, it's just that this whole thing has been weird.'

'Shae, I promise, just a bit longer.' He hugged me then got in the car. His horn honked into the night as he drove off.

'You didn't show him the picture, did you?' said Lexi, from behind.

I removed the image from my pocket and unfolded it. The creases were starting to distort the picture that I had folded and unfolded so many times already.

'I couldn't,' I sighed. 'I'm going to wait until the person calls again.'

'*If* they call,' she said.

'They'll call, I know it.'

Lexi leant against the porch. 'So, I guess I'm going to be an aunty.' She twisted her hair around her finger as she looked up toward the night sky.

'Aunty Lexi, that's crazy. Maybe I can be Aunty Shae?'

I didn't have any siblings so I would never really get the opportunity to be an aunty. Being an aunty to my cousin's kids would be the next closest thing.

'Aunty Shae has a nice sound to it,' said Lexi.

We grinned at one another and it helped ease the tension, for now.

Chapter 21

Music blared all around us as we sat in the roller-skating booth. Strobe lights flickered as a disco ball pasted dots across the bare cream walls. They flicked over Lexi, spotting her face as it spun around. The stale foot odour stench mixed with the strawberries and cream aroma coming from the smoke machine made for a pungent combination.

I pumped my fists in the air. 'Yay, roller-skating!'

'Are you sure you want to be here, Shae? We can go home if you want,' said Lexi.

'What? And miss my chance of carving it up on the rink?'

'Be serious. We don't have to stay,' she said.

'I think we both need to be doing something tonight. Especially after Aileen's news.'

'I still can't believe it. Little Miss Responsibility! If anyone was going to get pregnant ... ' Lexi ran her hands through her hair. 'Well, it wouldn't have been her.'

'She might be on the other side of the world, but she'll be okay, Lexie.'

'I know, but I feel weird about it for some reason. England is a long way away.'

'She's your big sister. Of course it's going to feel weird for a while. But you'll get used to the idea. You all will, especially your parents.' I grabbed her hand. 'Come on, let's skate!'

Lexi laughed at my exuberance. I was easily the world's worst roller-skater.

Out of nowhere a loud thud hit the barrier. 'Well, hello,' said Blake's friend, Grub.

'Keep your slimy hands off her,' warned Lexi.

'Come on sexy Lexi. You know you'll always be my favourite girl.' He grabbed her hand and waved it around.

She flicked his hand away. 'Don't touch me, or her.'

'Yeah, especially her,' said Blake, pointing at me. 'That's our cousin Shae.'

'No way!' Grub's eyes opened wider. 'I remember you. Wow, you've got … older.'

I gripped my chin as if deep in thought. 'And you've got … nope, haven't changed.'

Blake pulled his friend into a headlock. 'She's already worked you out, Grub.'

They wrestled each other while circling around on their wheels.

'Stop, I give in,' Grub yelled.

Blake gave him one last shove. 'Lexi, guess who's here?' He adjusted his hat backwards into position.

'Who?' Her eyes narrowed, immediately suspicious.

Blake wriggled his eyebrows.

'Just tell me who it is,' said Lexi.

'Nadine.' Blake grinned widely.

'Really, where?' Lexi scanned the place for her nemesis. 'I'll tell her what I think of her blonde highlight discount.'

I looked around, but it was too dark and the flashing lights made it hard to see.

'Lexi, don't you start anything with Nadine,' warned Blake.

'Why do you hate her so much?' I asked.

'That's a bit harsh! I don't hate Nadine, I just don't like her.'

'Well, I like her so I might go find her and catch up on old times,' said Blake with a grin.

'You mean perv on her from afar,' Lexi said.

Blake managed to look offended. 'Hey, I didn't just perv. We used to talk to each other as well, you know.'

Grub slapped him on the shoulder. 'Moaning in your dreams doesn't count mate.'

Blake shoved his friend off him. 'You wait and see. I'm gonna tee up a date before the night's through.'

'A date with Nadine? Eww.' Lexi screwed up her nose. 'You must be desperate.'

Blake laughed at Lexi's insult, adjusted his cap again, and skated away.

'Better go pick up the broken pieces,' said Grub as he skated after Blake.

'Grub's harmless,' said Lexi. 'Him and Blake have been friends for years and he pretty much does whatever Blake says. Just don't encourage him or you'll never get rid of him.'

I laughed and it felt good.

Lexi fluffed her hair and scanned the crowd. 'Okay, let's skate!'

She wouldn't be happy now until she found Nadine. I shoved my foot into the smelly, hired skates and pulled the laces tight. I stood up and immediately my feet moved in opposite directions. I leant against the table and shuffled them back together.

I gripped Lexi's arm to keep balanced. Together we managed to get on the roller-skating rink. It was even slipperier so I gripped the rail and moved around the edge. Lexi stayed close then stopped suddenly.

'Shae, look.' She tugged my arm.

I nearly toppled over. 'Don't do that.'

'There she is! Bloody Nadine'

In the distance stood an older, even prettier version of the Nadine I remembered from next door. Her hair was almost silver it was so blonde. It made Lexi's blonde locks look yellow. Nadine waved at Lexi enthusiastically.

'Better go say hello,' Lexi mumbled through gritted teeth.

She skated off and I was left to shuffle my way toward them.

'Lexi, it's been too long,' said Nadine, leaning across the low wall to hug her.

Lexi returned the embrace. 'Oh my gosh it's been way too long,' Lexi gushed. 'You remember Shae, my cousin?'

'Of course I remember!'

Nadine reached across to hug me. I lost my balance and accidentally head-butted her nose.

'I'm so sorry. I've got the worst balance.'

Lexi covered the smile on her face.

'Don't worry about it,' said Nadine, patting her nose.

'Here's your drink.' Blake passed a can of soft drink to Nadine. 'Looks like you two found each other.'

'Yeah, we did, but I'm surprised you're actually talking to Nadine,' said Lexi. 'Shouldn't you be spying on her like you used to?'

Nadine laughed. 'We're not little kids anymore, Lexi. Blake doesn't need to spy now.'

Lexi rolled her eyes as Nadine smiled at Blake.

'Need some help, girls?' asked Simon as he skated past and spun in a circle a couple of times.

'Look at you, what a show off,' I teased.

'I could give you some handy tips,' he said.

'Nah, Shae prefers the slow lane,' said Kai, stopping in front of me.

He grabbed Lexi and pulled her toward him. Lexi kissed Kai in a slow, deliberate display of public affection. They eventually broke apart and she smiled at Nadine.

'It was great seeing you, Nadine.' She pulled Kai away behind her.

I followed behind, but had no chance of keeping up with Lexi. They stayed close to me anyway as we circled around the edge.

'You can go faster, Simon. There is no hope of me becoming a champion skater,' I said. 'This is as good as I get.'

'Come on, Simon,' said Kai, shoving him. 'Race you.'

They skated off ahead. After a few laps my confidence increased, but not enough to move off the wall. Lexi stayed but I could tell she was itching to show off in front of Kai. An exit was coming up so I seized my chance.

'You go and skate. I'll be fine,' I said to her.

'Are you sure?' Her face lit up.

'Absolutely! Have fun.'

Lexi didn't need any more encouragement and pushed off. I veered off at the exit and stepped up just as my other foot shot backwards. I was about to do the splits when hands grabbed me. I collapsed into them, grateful. I looked up to see crinkled dark eyes smiling down at me.

'Falling for me I see,' said Callen.

'Stalking me I see.'

He laughed. The sound made my tummy flip flop. He took a moment before releasing me.

'Thanks for saving my body from certain bruising,' I said. 'Lexi made me come. You probably saw her whizzing around out there.'

'Nope, but I saw you.'

I blushed.

'Let me help get you to the table in one piece,' said Callen.

He curled his arm around my waist as we made our way toward the table. I tried to ignore the warmth of his hand, but it burned through the fabric. I looked back once at the roller- skating rink.

Lexi whirled by and saw who I was with. Her mouth made an 'O' shape before breaking into a grin and giving me a thumbs up. Simon followed closely behind. His smile shrunk when he saw who I was with. Instead, he gave me a small awkward wave and sped off past Lexi. I didn't want Simon to get the wrong idea, but I wasn't sure what that reaction was for. Did it have something to do with me and him? Or with me and Callen?

Chapter 22

I managed to make it from the rink in one piece and plonked on the seat. I removed the plastic wheels of death as Callen watched on.

'I had you picked for someone with more balance,' he said.

'Give me two wheels any day. Four wheeled shoes suck.'

He laughed and I realised I liked the sound of it.

'You can sit down if you want,' I offered.

He dropped into the seat across from me. His long legs knocked against mine. I moved across to make room. Soon they were touching again, but I didn't move this time.

'Why aren't you out there?' I asked.

The music pounding made it difficult to talk.

Callen leaned across the table. 'Not really my thing.'

'Then why'd you come?'

'Lexi mentioned you were coming.'

'So, you are stalking us,' I said.

'Just one of you.'

My cheeks warmed again. 'Hey, thanks again for the lift home. I got some answers, but now I've got a lot more questions as well.'

He leaned in even closer. The pop music was pumping at a rock concert level making it nearly impossible to have a conversation without yelling.

'I'm still trying to sort through some things,' I explained.

'You'll work it out,' he said, covering my hands with his.

I smiled. 'I seem to be saying thanks to you a lot lately.'

There was a thud behind me. Callen removed his hands from mine, his face drawn tight. I looked behind me and saw Kai standing there. Callen stood up and gripped the table. The two eyeballed each other as tension radiated between them like heat from a summer fire.

'Hi, Callen,' said Lexi, oblivious to it all.

'What's he doing here?' Kai said.

'I invited him,' she said.

'What for? He's nothing but a piece of garbage,' said Kai.

'Kai, just let it go,' said Simon.

'Listen to your mate, Kai,' said Callen.

There was a barrier between the two, but it wouldn't be enough to stop either one if they started something. I stood up, creating an extra obstacle between them.

'Callen's a friend so back off, Kai.'

'Of course.' He shook his head. 'Should've known you'd have a friend like this loser.'

Lexi whacked his shoulder. '*Kai*! Cut it out.'

Kai's face was set like stone as he ignored everyone around him, except for one person. Callen gently moved me aside. The testosterone in the space was through the roof. Both guys were like wild dogs getting ready to defend their territory. Wave a piece of meat in front of them and they would charge.

'What's your problem?' Callen glared at Kai.

They stood eye to eye, both tall and unflinching. Kai's cropped hair made his head square and menacing. Callen's stance meant he was not backing down.

'You shouldn't be here,' said Kai.

'It was a public place the last time I checked,' said Callen, not giving an inch.

'Does your little girlfriend know what happened last time we met in a public place?' Kai asked.

Callen's gaze flitted to me before landing back on Kai. 'Are you threatening me?'

I grabbed Callen's hand. 'You know what? We were just leaving. Callen's giving me a lift home. Lexi, can you tell Blake?'

I ignored the hurt look on Simon's face and tried to pull Callen behind me. He glared at Kai one last time before turning to leave. My heart pounded. I hoped Kai didn't follow us. With any luck Simon and Lexi would talk him into staying. I kept walking, tugging Callen behind me. We emerged into the warm summer night. The music dimmed as the door closed behind us. After a few steps I was still holding Callen's hand.

'Oh, sorry,' I said, dropping it.

'Don't you want to hold my hand?'

'Yes, I mean, no! I mean … ' I sighed.

Callen pushed some hair behind my ear. 'You didn't have to do that. I was handling it.'

I shrugged. 'Any excuse to get out of roller skating.'

We started walking toward the car park. It was full of all different makes and models. I searched for Callen's but couldn't see it.

'Thanks for sticking up for me back there. It's been a while since anyone has done that.'

'No problem. You weren't doing anything wrong. Kai's the loser, not you. I seriously can't work out what my cousin sees in him.'

'I have to agree with you about that. She could do much better than that moron.'

I stopped walking and looked around the car park again.

'Where's your car?' I asked.

'Why?'

'Because I just told Lexi you were giving me a lift home.'

'The only lift I can give you is over my shoulders.' He bent down to pick me up.

I pushed him away squealing. 'Are you crazy? Where's your car?'

'It's a nice night so I walked.' He shrugged. 'I can *walk* you home.'

He reached for my hand and I didn't resist. We left the car park and headed towards home. There was a small breeze that did little to cool me down. I looked up at Callen and caught him watching me. It sent a thrill through me, but I tried not to let it show.

'Are you staying at your pop's all summer?' I asked.

'My parents said it would be good for him, and for me.'

I nodded although not really understanding his cryptic response. He must have picked up my confusion.

'It's complicated,' he said.

I nodded. 'Hmm, I know that feeling.'

'Do you want to talk about it?' he asked.

I shook my head. 'Not tonight. Let's just keep it simple.'

Callen turned to face me. He reached out for my other hand and held them both tight.

'I know you don't know me that well,' he said. 'But you can trust me.'

I didn't know if that were true. Sondra's warning was brutal. *'Don't believe a word that comes out of that lying snake's mouth.'* And what did Kai mean about the last time they met in a public place?

'Callen, I … ' There were so many things left unexplained, for both of us. Yet something about him drew me in. I wanted to know more.

His eyes searched mine. A set of long thick lashes surrounded them. 'Have you ever been to Magnetic Island?' he asked.

I shook my head, confused by the sudden change in conversation.

'Would you like to come with me? There's something I'd love to show you.'

A day with Callen alone again. 'I'd like that,' I said.

'So, it's a date, for real this time?'

I nodded. Music broke the silence as *doof, doof* sounds got louder and the bass pulsed through my body. Brakes squealed, then the car did a U turn and pulled up alongside us. A guy wearing a baseball cap high on his head got out. He left the door open.

'What are you doing in a place like this?' His voice was gruff and his face serious. Then he grinned and opened his arms wide.

Callen moved toward him and was pulled in for a hug of sorts. 'Hey, Timmo. What's happening?'

The driver emerged and lifted his head slightly. 'Hey man, what's up?'

'Fish, how are you doin'?' Callen's tone was light, but his face remained serious.

Fish walked closer and repeated the half hug, fist-slamming action with Callen.

'You should be more careful walkin' round here at night, my friend,' said Timmo. 'Specially with someone so cute.'

'Ease up, Timmo! Shae's with me, geez,' said Callen.

Timmo patted Callen on the shoulder. 'Relax man, I'm just teasing ya. We both know I have more luck with the ladies.'

Callen shook his head with a smirk. 'Your natural charm always wins them over, right?'

Timmo laughed. 'You bet it does!'

'Haven't seen you for a while,' Fish said, all smiles gone.

'I'm still around. Been busy helping my Pop, that's all.'

'We miss you, bro. You always seem to be busy,' Timmo said. 'Ain't been the same lately.'

Callen looked at Fish who turned his head away.

'Things change, Timmo. That's just the way it is. Ain't nobody's fault,' said Callen.

'Maybe, but mates don't change, man. And we're mates. We gotta hang out soon, all of us together, alright?'

Callen nodded. He stepped toward Timmo and half-hugged him. Fish held up his hand. It waited alone in the air momentarily until Callen grabbed it. They did a fist bump before Fish walked back to the car. He stopped to light a cigarette. The glow was like a firefly in the darkness.

Fish took a deep drag. 'Hey, Callen? Timmo's right.' He puffed the smoke out. 'We miss you. So umm, maybe when your Pop don't need you, we can hang out. Like old times.'

Callen shoved his hands into his pockets. 'Yeah, maybe.'

'Okay, well … take care,' he said. 'It can be dangerous out at night. You know how it gets sometimes.'

Fish climbed back inside the car and Timmo waved a final goodbye. Callen rolled back and forth on his feet. Both car doors slammed and tyres spun as a trail of music blaring was left in its wake. Callen took a moment before he turned to look at me. He was pale in the moonlight and all traces of humour were gone.

'Friends of yours?' I asked, lightly.

'They were once. But not so much anymore.'

He took my hand again, tighter, and we walked the remainder of the way home in silence. So much for keeping things simple.

Chapter 23

The next morning Uncle Kevin woke everyone up early. He had a camping trip planned for all of us. After the phone call from Aileen, I didn't think we'd still be going, but Aunty Liz had insisted. The car ride was quiet for a change. Aunty Liz seemed better about the news this morning, but had made it clear she did not want to talk about it.

Lexi poked Blake. 'Tell us, Romeo, did you score a date last night?'

'As a matter of fact, I did.'

'Who's dating my handsome young man?' asked Aunty Liz.

'We're not dating, Mum, and it's Nadine from next door.'

'Good for you, son,' said Uncle Kevin. 'But in light of recent events, should we have the birds and the bees talk?'

'Kevin!' said Liz.

'It was a joke, Liz.' He laughed.

'Well, it's not funny, not yet anyway. And you.' She turned to Blake. 'Take things slow, there's no need to rush anything. You can just … enjoy Nadine's company.'

'Personally, I think your taste in girls just took a nose dive,' said Lexi.

Secretly I gave Blake a thumbs up.

***

'We're here,' said Uncle Kevin, turning into the campground.

Groups of people were already set up, scattered around the powered and unpowered sites. Uncle Kevin parked in the designated spot. The beach could be seen from the camp site and it looked perfect. Once the engine cut out, it was organised chaos. Everyone pitched in to help.

'Throw me the hammer, Shae,' Blake ordered. 'This ground is like a rock.' He banged the tent peg in as I grabbed a handful more ready to pass to him.

Aunty Liz and Lexi unpacked the car. It bulged with camping mats, chairs, food, and clothes. Lexi opened the back door and sleeping bags spilt onto the ground. Uncle Kevin pulled off the net covered trailer to reveal the barbeque and boogie boards.

'Hey, Lexi, are you going to be the leader, or will I?' I said, remembering the game we played as kids.

'Pity Aileen's not here. There's nobody to try and lose,' said Blake.

'She hardly joined in anyway,' said Lexi. 'Too busy reading her book.'

I continued passing pegs to Blake as he pounded them in.

Uncle Kevin inspected our work. 'Don't bang them all the way in. They'll never come out.'

We threaded the poles between the canvas holes. The tent was a camouflage colour, like an old army tent. It was a huge structure with a bedroom at each end and a living room dividing the two. It had to be big with a family of six and they could always squeeze me in. The only time I ever went camping was when I stayed with my cousins.

'No comfort, no stay.' That was my mother's motto. Paying to lie on the dirt was not on her list of things to do. We always stayed in apartments with the comforts of home, especially the bed.

Blake, Lexi and I threw our stuff up one end of the tent and set up our sleeping areas.

'Shae can go in the middle,' said Lexi.

'No way! Then I would have to put up with the both of you wiggling and snoring.'

'I don't snore,' said Lexi, offended.

'How would you know? You're asleep,' said Blake. 'Besides, I'm sleeping in the swag.'

When we were little all of us kids were shoved up one end. Nobody wanted to miss out by getting stuck with the adults. As we got older, Aileen moved down and Dale pitched a tent for himself.

Once everything was unpacked, we grabbed our towels and went to the beach. The blue sky stretched out with no end to it. Other families had claimed their patch of sand along the beachfront. Squeals of laughter rang out across the waterfront. A game of beach cricket between some little kids was already in action. It was always the first thing Dale and Blake made us play when we were younger. I bowled better than I batted.

I laid my towel down and kicked off my thongs.

'Kai and Simon are coming down after lunch,' said Lexi. 'I think Simon likes you.'

I rolled my eyes. 'I spent an afternoon with him because you ditched me to smooch in the bushes. That's it.'

'What bushes? I hope that's all that was going on in the bushes,' said Blake.

'Oh yeah? What about Castle Hill the other day?' she said.

I could tell she regretted mentioning it as soon as the words were out of her mouth. Her eyes flew to Blake, then back to me.

'What bushes?' Blake repeated.

Lexi thumped his arm and ran toward the water. 'I don't kiss and tell!'

She dived in without hesitation. There's the Lexi I knew. Brave, confident, carefree. So why did she let Kai boss her around?

'She wasn't really in the bushes with Kai, was she?' Blake's hands sat on his hips.

'Are you always so protective these days?' I teased.

'You've met Kai, right?'

'Good point, but Lexi's a big girl now,' I said. 'She can handle herself.'

'I know, it's just, Lexi had a tough year.'

I paused, caught off guard by his statement. 'What happened to her?'

'It doesn't matter. It's just, she's my little sister so of course I'm gonna worry about her.'

I dropped the topic, for now. 'Come on, let's go in,' I urged.

We walked to the water's edge and it lapped at my ankles. Lexi was already out deep. She beckoned us to join her. I hesitated for a moment, but Blake gripped my hand and pulled me behind him. I had no choice but to follow. A couple more steps and I lost my balance. I squealed with shock and delight as the wave crashed against me and I sank beneath the water. I jumped up and tried to push Blake over. He was too quick and dove beneath the surf. We moved out further, closer to the waves. They weren't that big, perfect for floating.

'What are you going to do this year?' I flicked some water at Blake.

He finished high school last year but had been pretty quiet about his plans. He ducked under the next wave.

Good avoidance technique. 'Well?' I asked, not letting him off that easy.

'I dunno. Something will come up.'

'You applied for Uni, right?'

He shrugged.

'Blake? Please tell me you applied.'

'Why? Because that's what I should do?'

I nodded. 'Well yeah, actually. You've got the brains so why not?'

'I'm not like Aileen and Dale. They always knew what they wanted. They've always been sure where they were headed. Aileen into Science and Dale into Accounting, easy. They never chopped and changed when they were deciding.'

'Don't you want to do sports physio?' I asked.

'Yeah, I did. But now I'm not so sure. Plus, you need good grades for that, and mine were not great.'

I waited a beat before pushing. 'Did you at least apply?'

He nodded. 'But I'm not holding my breath. I know I won't get an offer.'

The misery was clear on his face. Blake was always on Lexi's case about getting things done. Now here he was, lost and unsure.

'Do your parents know?' I asked.

He shook his head. 'You can't say anything, not even to Lexi. Especially to Lexi. She'll just blab it out to the folks.' He shrugged as if resigned to his fate. 'They'll all find out soon.'

'But summer will be finished and then what? I think they'll notice if you keep hanging around the house every day,' I said.

'Will they? I'm not the one they've ever had to worry about and I don't want them to start now. Especially with Aileen's news.'

'Blake, you have to talk to them.'

He held his hand in front of my mouth to shush me but I swatted it away.

'Seriously, Shae, something will come up. It'll work out, it always does. I'm not worried, so you don't need to be.' He flicked my nose then disappeared under the water, ending the conversation.

He swam toward Lexi, then pulled her legs out from under her. She came up gasping and spluttering and retaliated. Back and forth they wrestled to push each other under. Lexi climbed up onto

Blake's back. He twirled her around then dumped her in the water. I watched them with love, but also a smidge of sibling envy. My parents only had me.

I asked them once why they never had another child. Dad said one gift from above was enough.

Chapter 24

Kai and Simon arrived after lunch as Lexi had planned. They wanted to show us a waterfall that was nearby. I wished Lexi had never made that stupid comment about Simon liking me. The space was cramped in the back, even with the gap between us.

'I don't think your brother likes me,' said Kai, pulling into the Jourama Falls car park.

'Don't worry about Blake, he's just … Blake,' said Lexi, winding her window up.

'Have you been here before?' Simon asked me.

I shook my head.

'The waterfall's beautiful to look at, but the swimming hole is freezing.'

'Hey, sorry about leaving early the other night,' I said. 'Thought it was the best thing to end whatever was going on between those two.'

'It's no problem, besides, you're here now,' he smiled.

We took our bags from the boot and crossed the camping ground. There were a few tents set up but not many people around. We walked toward the south end of the camp ground. It was extra muggy today. My singlet clung to me from the drive here. I hoped there were no sweat marks, *eww*. Simon led us to a water hole surrounded by gum trees. It spread out wide with reeds bordering the edge. The water was surprisingly clear and it was easy to see the bottom. That relaxed me knowing there was no chance any eels, or fish or any other slimy creatures could nibble around my feet.

'I don't know about going in there. How cold is it?' I asked, trying to dip a toe in without committing the whole foot.

'Come in, it'll cool you down,' said Simon. He pulled off his top and dove into the water.

He reappeared and flicked the water from his head. 'You have to come in, Shae. It's beautiful!'

'Yeah, live a little,' said Kai.

Lexi threw her bag on the ground and undressed. Kai watched her then waited until she was poised on the edge before removing his top. I looked away before he caught me spying on him. I just didn't trust that guy.

Lexi walked into the water until she was submerged from her neck down. Her head looked like it was floating, detached from her body.

'Come on, Shae, don't be a baby,' she teased.

I folded my clothes on top of the bag and treaded carefully toward the edge. Simon dipped below the water, as though I didn't just catch him staring at me. I adjusted my bikini and crept my way in. It was icy cold and I gasped as it got deep, quicker than I expected.

Lexi let out a big cheer when I was in up to my neck. Her arms draped around Kai's middle who sat on the edge. He leant down and whispered something in her ear. I looked away. As if I cared what he was saying. Then Kai cracked open a can of beer. He seemed to skull half the thing before taking a breath. He handed the can to Lexi who took it and finished it off with a burp. What was she doing drinking in the middle of the day?

Simon flicked me with water.

'Hey, no splashing,' I said. Once he stopped, I floated around the water taking in the green surrounds. The sunlight filtered through in patches but the shade was a welcome relief.

'How do you know about this place?' I asked Simon.

'My dad brings me here with my two brothers sometimes. We camp under the stars with our swags. On the really hot days we swim until our skin is wrinkled.'

'So, you're close to your dad?' I asked.

'Yeah, why? You sound surprised.'

'It's just, I just got the impression the other day that ... well you said it can be rough at home.'

'Ahh. You thought 'rough' as in, got beat up?' he said, understanding.

I was immediately embarrassed for jumping to conclusions. 'Sorry.'

'My dad's such a pushover, he'd never hurt us,' said Simon. 'It's just that when he's gone, my mum can spiral. She takes antidepressants, but some days are harder than others. Some days she can't even get out of bed.' He shrugged and I knew he wasn't looking for sympathy.

'When that happens, Dad tells me I have to step up and be the man. Help out with my brothers and stuff, you know. So, that's what I do.'

'Of course, you would help out,' I said. 'I told you already, you're a nice guy.'

'That's true.' He moved closer to me. 'I do remember you saying something like that about me.'

I swam backwards to put some space between us. 'How old are your brothers?'

'John is nine and Seb is twelve. Mum says they look up to me with the old man being away so much.'

'Any sisters?' I asked.

He shook his head. 'If I did, I'd be like Blake and hate any guy that went near her.'

'Yeah, Blake's a good guy.' I gave Kai an appraising look. 'Unlike some.'

'You really don't like Kai, do you?'

'I know he's your friend, but there's just something about him that annoys me.'

Simon changed the subject. 'What about you? Any brothers or sisters? A hidden twin somewhere?'

I shook my head. 'Nope, just me. I've always wished I had a brother or sister. Instead, I got the best cousins to hang out with. It's not the same, but I reckon it's pretty close.'

Somehow Simon had managed to drift close to me again.

'Well, I've definitely cooled off,' I said, climbing out of the water hole.

'Do you want to walk up and see the waterfall?' asked Simon.

'Sure.'

We called out to the other two who followed reluctantly. I noticed Kai scoop up several empty cans. How many did they drink? I put my sarong and singlet back on. Lexi lost her balance as she pulled on her denim shorts. She didn't bother with a singlet, instead leaving her bikini top exposed.

'Let's go see the beautiful waterfall,' she said, giggling.

Kai nudged her and they laughed at some shared joke. Simon took the front and I followed. Lexi and Kai lagged behind. It was only a 3km round trip but after a while the distance between us and them grew wide. The rocky path meant I had to watch my step more carefully. We crossed over a small bridge where the water ran fast downstream. Simon waited for me to catch my breath and take in the tranquil view. Then we continued to hike upward, although Simon slowed the pace a bit. After a while we came to an area that was full of different sized boulders. Some were so big it would be impossible to climb up on top. Others would be easier to navigate. Some water ran though the base of them clustered together, but not enough to swim in. From there I got a glimpse of the waterfall in the distance. I kept checking behind me but could see no sign of Lexi and Kai.

I puffed my way up the final stretch, careful to step carefully along the rock filled path. Finally, the viewing platform loomed in the distance. I rested against the rail and took in the spectacular view. The hike had been worth the effort. It wasn't just one waterfall but a collection of four waterfalls stretched over the rock face that flowed from left to right and back again. Greenery grew out of the rockface to add to the beauty in front. The water cascaded down, and the roar was loud as it hit the gully below and winded downwards. We were up high and the barrier did little to ease my nerves as I stepped back, realising just how high up we were. The greenery spread around us as cockatoos broke free and made a racket as they flew away. The silence settled once again as we took in the view. Before long, footsteps get louder, closer.

'Wow, it's beautiful,' said Lexi, emerging from the path.

Kai was close behind her.

'It's so pretty.' Lexi tried to climb up on the safety rail to perch herself on top, but slipped, falling forward.

'Careful!' Simon steadied her.

She turned around laughing, unfazed. She tried to focus on me. Her eyes had a glassy texture, as though she had just woke up. Kai dropped his arms around her shoulders.

'I told you it would be awesome,' he whispered in her ear.

I raised my eyebrows at Simon. *What the hell is going on?* He broke my gaze.

'Lexi, are you okay?' I asked. 'How much did she drink?' I asked Kai.

'She's fine,' Kai slurred.

'Only had a couple,' said Lexi, holding up two, then three then four fingers 'Hey, you can have some. There's more in the car.'

She reached out to a tree, plucking a leaf from its branch.

'It's all so pretty. Light green, dark green. Like a bean!' She twirled the leaf in her fingers.

A boom of thunder burst from the sky. Dark clouds had rolled in and we were directly below them. The sky opened up and the wet season arrived without warning. Plump, heavy rain splattered about. Lexi squealed as she tried to catch the raindrops.

'Move it, Lexi,' I said.

We scrambled to grab our bags and ran down the path. Solid ground became muddy as more thunder rumbled from above. Lexi slipped and I caught her elbow. We stumbled along the track, but the rocks had become slippery and it was difficult to move quickly. The sky became even darker until eventually we emerged off the track and at the campground.

'Keep moving,' yelled Simon.

We made it to the shelter of the car, exhausted, drenched and muddy. Kai fumbled, trying to find the keys before unlocking it. We all scrambled inside. Lexi laughed hysterically from the front seat. Her hair was strapped flat and droplets fell from the ends.

I pulled out my towel to dry off. My clothes were stuck to my skin and it wasn't long before the towel was soaking wet and useless.

'Great weather for camping,' I muttered.

'So intense, for sleeping in tents,' said Lexi, laughing. 'Get it? Intense for *in tents*?'

'Buckle up, baby,' said Kai, adjusting the rear-view mirror.

'Wait!' I grabbed his arm. 'You can't drive if you've been drinking. Let me drive.'

'I can still drive, sweetheart.'

I shook my head. 'Then I'll walk.'

Kai shrugged. 'Enjoy the long, wet walk home.'

I opened the door. 'It'll be safer out there walking than in here with you driving drunk.'

Simon reached over and pulled the door shut. 'I'll drive.'

Kai glared at me before handing the keys to Simon.

'Do you even have your license?' I asked.

'Nope, but I can drive. Dad taught me in case of an emergency,' Simon said.

'You better hope there's no cops on the road,' said Kai.

'You better hope Blake doesn't find out you're giving his sister alcohol,' I replied.

'Whatever.' He turned to face toward the window.

Lexi was already curled up asleep in the front seat, oblivious to her moron boyfriend.

Chapter 25

It was the first morning back since camping. Lexie and I had managed to avoid each other without too much effort. I poured some cereal into a bowl then plonked down at the table. The bubbles crackled in my mouth.

'Enough with the crunching!' said Blake, throwing down the newspaper. 'At least turn the radio on so I don't have to listen to you.'

'Get out of bed on the wrong side, did ya?' I crunched extra loud with my mouth open.

His face crumpled. 'Aww geez, I'm sorry.'

Blake never got cross at me, or anyone for that matter. I looked at the page he was reading. *"First round offers only days away."* I scanned the article about some guy who was set to be dux at his school and was sure to get into medicine.

'Blake, you're going to have to talk to them sooner or later.'

'Later works fine with me.' He ran his hand through his hair then sat his cap back on top.

'Besides, you're one to talk. What's up with you and Lexi?' He leaned back in the chair with his arms crossed.

'Nothing.'

'Come off it, Shae. You two have hardly said a word to each

other since the waterfall.'

'Sure, we have,' I said.

'"*Can you tell your sister to move?*" doesn't count as you having a conversation with her. I'm not stupid, Shae. What happened?'

I sighed. 'You'd have to ask her.'

'Ask her what?' Lexi appeared in the doorway.

He looked between the two of us and pushed his chair out with a huff. 'Fine, but whatever happened, you two need to work it out.'

He dumped his bowl in the sink with a clang and left us to it. The kitchen shrunk. I wasn't sure what to say to Lexi. First smoking, now getting drunk during the day time. What else had she been doing that I didn't know about?

Lexi yanked out a box of cereal and slammed it on the bench. I shoved another mouthful in, but it tasted like wet cardboard so I emptied the remainder in the bin.

'Don't leave on my account,' said Lexi. 'Then again, I sure don't need a babysitter.'

'Seems to me like you do,' I said.

'What the hell does that mean? I'm older than you.'

'*Then act it!*'

She flinched. Guilt washed over me, but I refused to apologise like I normally would. Somehow, I always managed to be the one that gave in with Lexi. Most of the time I indulged her. We all did. Maybe that was the problem. *'Ahh Lexi, you know how she is.'*

Perhaps everyone had been letting her get away with things for too long. Enough was enough. Anything could have happened the other day. She nearly fell off the safety rail ledge. Her boyfriend was going to drive drunk and she didn't even care! Worse still, I didn't think drinking during the day was a new thing for either of them.

'What were you thinking at the waterfall? Was it to impress that idiot boyfriend?'

She folded her arms across her chest. 'He's not an idiot.'

'He sure isn't the kind you want to keep.'

'You don't know him. You don't know a thing about him,' she said, her face scrunching up.

'I know he gave his girlfriend alcohol and nearly let her fall off a cliff.'

'That's such bullshit.'

'*Simon had to grab you!*'

She shoved her chair out and stood up. 'Kai wouldn't have let me fall.'

'Oh really? Hate to tell you, but safety wasn't at the top of his priorities when he was going to *drive* his friends' home while he was *under the influence*. What kind of person does that, Lexi?'

'Nothing happened, so calm down.'

This was not the cousin I had grown up with. She had changed, and not for the better.

'Who are you?' I demanded. 'The Lexi I know wouldn't put up with that kind of crap.'

Lexi stormed outside, slamming the sliding door behind her.

Grrr! I gripped the table. Well, that went as bad as possible. This arguing was stupid. We never argued. I tried to remember Blake's words and his reluctance to tell me more at the beach. *'It's just Lexi had a tough year…'* Whatever had caused this change in Lexi was serious. It had to be more than Kai. But what? She'd come after me if it was the other way around. She wouldn't give up on me, so I couldn't give up on her.

After a moment I went outside looking for her. She sat on the edge of the pool with her legs curled up. Her shoulders shook and my heart tightened with guilt. I shouldn't have yelled, but the stunt at the falls was even dumber than at the Weir.

'Lexi,' I said, softly.

She sniffed. 'Leave me alone.'

I created some space between us and dangled my feet in the water.

After a while I spoke up. 'Do you remember when we were younger and we'd gang up on Aileen? We'd go out of our way to annoy her! Change her bookmark around, leave the top off her nail polish, that sort of stuff.' I laughed. 'She used to get so mad and tell us to grow up,'

Lexi wiped her nose with her hand. 'She always thought she was so mature being the oldest girl.'

'We were happy being the youngest because we got away with stuff,' I continued. 'But we can't do that anymore. Get away with stuff.'

'Don't I know it,' she said.

I was hardly the one that should be giving her a lecture. As long as she knew I cared and that she could confide in me, that's all that mattered.

'Do you want to tell me what's going on? You've been smoking, drinking beer, and whether you agree or not, your boyfriend is a loser.'

'Stop, Shae, I get it! Geez, you sound just like Aileen.' A small smile appeared on her face.

Being called Aileen was the worst insult we could throw at each other growing up. We loved her, but she was demanding.

Lexi adjusted the purple sunglasses on her face. 'You like?'

'I like *all* your sunnies.'

'I'm a collector, what can I say?'

There was another long pause before I tried again. 'Why don't you tell me what's happened,' I said. 'Stop avoiding it.'

She took a deep breath and wrapped her arms around herself. 'Last year I went out with this guy, Tyson. He enrolled halfway through the year. He was Mr. Popularity from the moment he started at Kirwan. All the girls liked him. He was cute, friendly, and funny, so of course I did my usual thing and got his attention. He had this way of talking to me like I was the only one around. As though he really did care about me.

143

'Then one night at a party we were kissing and stuff. We'd already hooked up a few times. He was a *really* good kisser. Mostly that's all we had done up to then, except this night his hands were wandering everywhere. At first it was fun, exciting, but he kept trying to go further. He coaxed me into one of the bedrooms. I told him I wasn't going to sleep with him. He said it didn't matter, and that we could do other stuff. He had already taken his top off and kept trying to get me to take mine off.

'Eventually I was lying on the bed in my bra and skirt. We kept kissing and his hands kept wandering. Then he stopped and told me not to move. I remember hearing a zipper then a rustling sound. When he came back, he was completely naked. I tried not to freak out and he promised he just wanted to lie next to me, to see what our skin felt like together. We kept kissing, but no matter what I did I couldn't get him to slow down. I panicked then kneed him in the balls and got the hell out of there.

'Course he told everyone we had sex. That I liked all sorts of weird stuff. The rumours went on for weeks, months. His mates would say horrible things to me when I walked past. Mikayla stuck by me, of course, but some of my other friends, well, let's just say we're not friends any more.

'Blake wanted to kill him when he heard about it, but I begged him to leave it alone. Kai was the first guy who liked me after that, for me and not the rumours. He doesn't go to my school, so I figured he couldn't have heard the made-up lies about me. You might not believe it, but he can be sweet sometimes. He says things that make me feel good, that make me feel special. I know you don't like him, but I could do a lot worse.'

'Oh, Lexi, you could do a whole lot better as well.'

I put my arm around her and we sat like that for a while, comfortable with each other once again.

Chapter 26

Honk, honk. Blake tooted as he drove off, leaving us along the Strand.

'Come on! Let's get a good spot near the life guards,' said Lexi, grabbing my hand as she led me along the pathway.

A cyclist rang their bell as they swerved to avoid us.

'Sorry!' Lexi called after them.

We walked along and I looked out toward Magnetic Island. It reminded me of my date with Callen. Did he really mean it when he said he wanted us to go there?

'Will Kai be joining us?' I asked.

'I didn't invite him.'

I stopped walking, surprised by her admission. 'Why not?'

Lexi shrugged. 'I think I need some space.'

'Space can be a good thing.'

'Plus, he can be irritating,' she continued. 'I can't keep up with his mood swings sometimes. It's draining.'

'Then don't do it.'

'Don't do what?' she stopped walking.

'Don't try and keep up with them. You don't owe Kai your loyalty just because he whispered some nice things in your ear,' I said.

'It's not like that.'

'Just think about it, Lexi. Please?'

She adjusted her hair to hang over one shoulder and nodded.

We cut across the grass toward the beach. Picnic blankets and low camp chairs were scattered along the waterfront. We passed the water park for little kids. Squeals rang out as they splashed around the giant mushroom where water squirted out the base.

'*Shae!*' A voice cut through the playground noise.

'Hello *cutie*,' Lexi muttered as a guy jogged toward us.

His cap shaded his face and it took me a moment to recognize him. 'Oliver?'

He gave me a hug.

'Mr-I-don't-do-the-beach! What are you doing here?' I asked.

'I'm here for a week. Mum's helping my aunty look after her kids.'

'Really, why?'

'She had some operation and can't get around very good. I think I'm the live-in babysitter.' He shrugged.

Two young boys ran our way and crashed into Oliver. He scooped them up and twirled them around.

'This is Jye. This is James.' Oliver introduced us to his cousins.

'How do you tell them apart?' Lexi asked.

Both had the same cropped blonde hair and perfect dimples, like cherub angels with chubby cheeks.

'It's a colour by twin thing. We just have to remember what colour goes with which twin,' Oliver said. 'But even that doesn't always work.' He grabbed the boys and tickled their bellies. 'Especially when they switch their tops.'

They squealed and ran off. Lexi gave me a meaningful look as she nodded her head toward Oliver.

'Olly, this is my cousin, Lexi,' I introduced them. 'I'm staying with her for a while.'

Lexi took his offered hand with a big smile. 'I'm the *favourite* cousin.'

Oliver turned his attention back to me. 'So, how are you?'

Something in his tone was off. 'I'm fine, why?'

'It's none of my business,' he said, suddenly avoiding my gaze.

'What do you mean?'

'It's just my mum ran into yours before we left Airlie. She mentioned how you guys had to cancel your New Zealand trip,' he explained.

'Yeah, it was a last-minute thing,' I said.

He nodded, but I could tell he was hiding something.

'Olly, what else did she say?' I asked.

'Nothing, well, not much anyway.'

'Oliver?'

'I don't know, something about a family situation that had to be dealt with.' He looked around everywhere but at me.

My pulse quickened and I reached for my necklace. 'Did she explain the family situation?'

Oliver shook his head. 'It was probably just Mum gossiping. You know what she's like, so I'm sure it's not true.'

Everyone knew Olly's mother was a walking bulletin board. She made it her business to know everybody else's business.

'Olly, just spit it out. What's not true?' I demanded.

'Mum said your parents might be breaking up, but they're not, right? I mean you would know.'

The twins returned and charged into Oliver. He sprawled on the ground and the twins piled on top like a climbing frame. He managed to push them off and stood up.

'Shae, I'm really sorry,' Oliver said.

My brain ran through all the things I had uncovered this trip. Was it possible? 'Don't be silly. They're not breaking up. I mean, I would know, right? It's nothing. Just work stuff, that's what they told me.' I tried to squash the rising panic spreading throughout my body as my heart rate stepped up a notch. *Breathe Shae.*

'Yeah, of course it will be work stuff. That makes sense. Mum's always getting things wrong.'

The twins pushed and shoved Oliver again. They held a hand on either side and began a tug-o-war.

'Come on Olly, we wanna play,' Jye said.

'You better go,' I said.

Olly leant in and gave me a hug, squeezing tight.

The twins tugged on Oliver's arms again. 'Olly! Olly!' they chanted, dragging him away.

'Hey, Oliver,' I called out. 'Lexi's having a party tomorrow night. You should come.'

He grinned. 'Count me in. That has to be better than another movie night. I don't know how many more animated animals I can take!'

'Great, I'll text you the details.'

I waved as the twins took his full attention and he chased them across the playground.

'Thanks, cuz, nice invite,' said Lexi.

'You are my *favourite* cousin after all.'

Lexi wrapped her arm around my shoulder and gave me a squeeze. 'We can give the beach a miss if you want.'

'Nope. This isn't going to ruin our day. My parents aren't breaking up. That's just stupid.'

'Of course, it is. There's no way that's happening.'

But what about all that cash? Maybe it wasn't blackmail money but starting over money.

Lexi squeezed my shoulder one more time. 'Are you sure you want to stay?'

'Absolutely! Where are those hot lifeguards?'

Lexi pumped her fist in the air. 'Thatta girl!'

She led me to the beach and we set out the towels. I tried to let the waves wash out my worries, except they only crashed louder in my mind.

Chapter 27

Blake dropped us home later that afternoon on his way to work. Occasionally he brought home new creations to try from the pizzeria where he worked. Vegetarian with meat was the best combination. It meant all the good stuff on one slice.

At the beach I tried to push away Olly's comments about my parents, but they had continued to surface all afternoon. Why would Mum confide in Olly's mum that there had been a family situation to deal with? Mum didn't even like Olly's mother and avoided her as much as possible. Everyone knew what a gossip she was. What else did Mum tell her that she hadn't told me? Her own daughter.

Lexi nudged me and pointed next door. As if I wasn't already hyper aware of Callen washing his car.

'Hi, Callen!' Lexi called out as she headed inside, conveniently leaving us alone.

Callen turned the hose off and strode across the grass. 'How was the beach?'

'How did you know?'

'I think it was the sarong that gave it away.'

'It was great,' I lied, thinking about the conversation with Oliver.

His eyes narrowed. 'You're not very convincing.'

'Actually, I ran into a friend from school. He's staying in Townsville for the week.'

A flicker of something crossed Callen's face.

'He said something about my parents and it got to me.' My phone blared from inside the beach bag.

'You better answer that,' said Callen.

I dug around until I found it. 'Hello?'

'Shae?'

'Who's this?'

'I think you know who it is,' said the female caller.

I turned away from Callen. 'When are you going to tell me what I want to know?'

'I was going to call earlier, but some things got in the way,' she said.

'So, when?' I persisted.

I didn't think the woman on the phone was the woman in the picture, but what piece of the puzzle was she in this whole mess?

'Can we meet now?' she asked.

I looked around as if she might be on the footpath out the front of the house. 'Now? Where?'

'At the Billabong Sanctuary, out on the Bruce Highway.'

I hadn't been there since I was little girl.

'How will I know who you are?' I asked.

'I know who you are. I'll find you,' she said. 'And I promise I'll tell you everything.'

The phone disconnected. It echoed in my ear in time with my pounding heart. Finally, I was going to meet this mysterious caller. *But who is she?*

'Are you okay?' asked Callen.

I looked up at him, dazed from the brief but loaded conversation. The caller wanted to meet with me, and they had promised to tell me everything. Was I ready to hear it all?

'There's somewhere I need to be,' I said.

'I can give you a lift,' he offered.

'That would be great. I'll just get changed.'

I ran inside and threw on some shorts and a singlet. Things had gone from naught to warp speed. I was finally going to get some answers today.

'Where are you going?' Lexi caught me in the hallway.

'Umm, I'm going for a drive with Callen.' I knew if I told Lexi what I was really doing she would demand to come with me. And I needed to meet this person on my own.

She wagged her finger at me. 'You better share *all* the details about your drive when you get back.'

'I will, I promise.'

Lexi didn't know the details I just promised to share would have nothing to do with Callen and me.

Callen changed gears fast but smoothly, as we drove along the Bruce Hwy. I gripped the seat and tried not bounce my knees as we drove along. I hoped the caller didn't change their mind and leave before I got there. Maybe they were as nervous as me. The more I thought about the image and replayed the voice from the phone call, the more I was sure they were two different people.

'Who was the mystery caller?' Callen broke the silence.

'I don't know.'

'That's okay, you don't have to tell me.'

'It's not that,' I said. 'I really don't know who they are.'

'You mean you're meeting someone you've never met?' His voice rose. 'Why? Who are they?'

'There are some other things I found out, after the road trip.'

I explained the photo that came in the post. I told him about the emails between Mum and Karen. I shared everything that had happened, and the more I talked, the more distant he became.

'I'm trying not to jump to conclusions, but it's a bit hard not to,' I said. Callen had seen the text messages. He had already jumped to the conclusion that Dad was having an affair.

Callen still didn't respond to my revelations. His face remained blank, passive. I didn't want a lecture from him about meeting a stranger, but I also didn't want indifference to my situation.

'Not that you care, obviously,' I mumbled, embarrassed by my blubbering. Here I was beginning to think maybe he was different and I could trust him. But his lack of response suggested otherwise. I turned away from him and crossed my arms. The silence between us seemed to go on for ages before Callen finally spoke.

'I do care, Shae. Trust me, I do. It's just, there's some things about me you should know.'

'Unless you're a private detective in your spare time, there's nothing I need to know at the moment.' I angled my knees toward the window, away from him. Still mad that I had just spilt my guts and he had nothing to say about it.

'I wasn't bike riding with friends that day at the Strand,' he said in a rush.

He turned into the Billabong Sanctuary and cut the engine. An uneasy silence settled inside the car. He had already been given a chance to tell me the truth about that day and he hadn't. Would he tell me the whole story today?

Callen gripped the wheel. 'If you can be so open with me now, then I want to be honest with you as well.'

'I'm listening.' I pulled on my necklace waiting for him to speak. What if I didn't like what he said?

'I wasn't riding with friends that day at the Strand,' he repeated. He looked up, vulnerable. 'You don't seem surprised by what I just told you.'

Looks like it was time to come clean about what I saw that

day. 'I'm not surprised. I've known all along you weren't riding with friends,' I said.

'How could you know that?'

I wriggled in my seat. 'I saw you get off the bus.'

Callen winced. 'You knew all this time?'

'I only knew you got off the bus. My mum explained why you might have been on it in the first place. And I'd heard some rumours before we met.'

I remembered the gossip from Mikayla passed on to Lexi who passed it on to me. *He was thrown out of his last school for beating some guy to death.* The violent rumours didn't match the Callen I was starting to know. And like.

'There are rumours about me?' he said.

'There are *some* rumours, but nobody is probably even talking about them anymore.'

'Easy for you to say!'

'Are you serious? Did you even listen to my story? The whole of Airlie Beach will be talking about my family at the moment thanks to Olly's mum!'

'You're right, I'm sorry. It's just the *Community Corrections* is like a storm cloud hanging over my head.' He banged the steering wheel.

'Don't you get it? None of that matters to me!' As I said the words, I realised they were true. The rumours, the warning from Sondra, none of that mattered because something deep inside told me he wasn't a bad person.

I reached for his hand. 'You should have told me earlier. I want to trust you, which means you need to trust me.'

'I do trust you, Shae. You're probably the only person I trust these days.'

He leant toward me and I had trouble breathing. Suddenly noise filled the car. Loud, blaring, block-your-ears noise.

'Damn it!' Callen adjusted the radio volume to low. 'Must have knocked it, sorry.'

I pushed back against the car seat, sure my face was bright red from what just nearly happened. It was suddenly stuffy in the car and I needed fresh air. Whether or not Callen was just about to kiss me was not the reason we were sitting in the Billabong Sanctuary carpark. There was other business that I needed to deal with today. How I felt about the near kiss would have to wait.

'Come on, let's go in,' I said, more confident than I felt. A stranger with answers to my questions was waiting just beyond that entry gate. What answers they had might determine the future of my family as I knew it.

Chapter 28

I looked around and wondered why the mystery caller chose to meet all the way out here. We walked toward the seating area. There were only a few people around this late in the day.

'I don't like this, Shae,' said Callen, for the third time. He looked around but like me, didn't know who to look for.

'It's a public place. It will be fine.'

A girl not much older than me watched us from the kiosk. She was familiar, but I couldn't place her. She walked toward us. 'Shae?'

I nodded. Callen tensed beside me.

'Hi, I'm Stella.'

It clicked where I had seen her before. 'Were you at the shopping centre the other day?'

She didn't deny it.

'Were you following me?' I asked.

'No! I was there, but I promise, it was just a coincidence that we were both there that day.'

I took a step backwards. Maybe this wasn't a good idea. This girl could be a psycho.

'I was walking past when I recognised you. I knew what you looked like from the internet,' she explained.

'You've been stalking me online?'

'No! Look I'm sorry for all the mystery, but I promise to explain everything if you just give me a chance.'

'Start talking then,' I said, tired of the covert operation.

Stella was nothing like the person I had been expecting. This girl was only older than me by a couple of years at the most. She was definitely not the woman in the photo.

Stella looked around. 'Come with me.'

Her gypsy skirt tinkled as she moved. Her light brown hair was pulled back, but it looked like it should be loose and free. Callen trailed behind us.

'Is he your bodyguard?' asked Stella.

'Something like that,' I said.

Stella smiled and I couldn't help but wonder if she was as nervous as me about this meeting. She didn't seem to be when she was making jokes about Callen. But maybe that was her way of dealing with nerves. I tended to shut down and stop talking.

We veered off the path following the sign that pointed toward the crocodiles.

'I work here,' said Stella. 'Actually, I volunteer, but hopefully one day I'll work here. I love the crocodiles. They're even older than dinosaurs! Did you know when they catch their prey, they take them into the water and roll them over and over and over. Each time their catch moves, they roll them again until they're dead. That's why they call it the death roll.'

I was unsure how to respond to this unexpected prehistoric beast lesson. The largest crocodile lazed in the sun, taking no notice of us.

'Come on, let's see the dingoes,' said Stella.

I looked at Callen, but he just shrugged. We passed the fenced dingo enclosure.

'Don't be fooled by them. They're nothing like pet dogs,' Stella said. 'They're territorial and can be very aggressive—'

'Let's cut the zoo lessons, Stella,' I interrupted. 'Who the hell are you and why did you send me that picture? What does it mean?'

'Which question should I answer?'

'All of them! Did you take the photo?'

She nodded slowly. 'I'd been suspicious for a while, but I needed to be sure.'

'Who's the woman in the picture?' I asked.

'My mother, Karen.' Stella sat down on the wooden bench seat. 'She wouldn't tell me anything when I asked, so that day I followed them.'

'Is my dad having an affair with her?' I blurted out the question, desperate for her to deny what I feared was true.

'They were, but it's been over for years.'

I released the breath I had been holding, thrown by Stella's response. *Over for years?*

'But the photo's recent,' I said.

'I needed proof after everything started to make sense.' Stella sighed. 'Do you know Mum, uhh, Karen, still tried to deny it after I confronted her?'

Stella scrunched her skirt into her hands then just as quickly released the material and patted it flat. It was suddenly obvious that I was not the only one to be angry and hurt by this whole mess.

'Why did Karen deny it? Because of your dad?'

This girl was making no sense. If the photo was recent, how could the affair be old?

'I've never met my dad. It wasn't Karen's affair all those years ago.'

Callen groaned behind me as pieces of the puzzle fell into place. The ground seemed to rush up towards me and ripple around. I looked closely at Stella, paused and unmoving as though waiting for me to catch up with what she was saying.

'Are you telling me … that you're my … sister?'

158

She nodded and I felt Callen curl his arm around my waist as my legs collapsed beneath me.

***

The radio filled the silence as we drove home. I couldn't look at Callen let alone imagine what he must have thought of my family. I had just met my sister. How many people have hidden siblings they're yet to meet? I had friends with half-brothers and step sisters. But nobody had ever found a brother or sister tucked away. Stella was so close to me all this time and yet neither of us had any idea the other was alive. Did my parents know about her existence? Or had they known all along and ignored her?

Callen pulled into the driveway. He pushed some frizzy hair out of my face. 'I'm just next door if you need anything.'

I nodded, then walked dazed inside the house. I flopped onto my bed, drained. *My sister.* This changed everything. My head spun with possibilities. Mum must know about the affair, but did she know there was a daughter involved? A love child. Did Dad know? Maybe that was what all the money was for. A lump sum payment for an absent parent.

'How was the drive?' Lexi stood in the doorway.

'I know who Karen is.' I stared straight ahead, unable to do any more than try to process the events of this afternoon.

'Karen? What's she got to do with driving with Callen?'

'He gave me a lift to meet the anonymous letter sender,' I said, quietly.

'Why didn't you tell me that's what you were doing?'

I sighed then patted my bed for Lexi to sit down. 'The woman in the photo is Karen and Dad definitely had an affair with her.'

'Had? So, it's finished?' she said.

'It's been finished for years.'

'Then what's with the emails and texts now?'

I took a deep breath. 'It's probably got something to do with my sister.'

'*What?*'

'She sent me the picture.' I filled Lexi in with the details.

'So, this chick, Stella, claims to be the love child from an affair between your dad and her mother, twenty years ago.'

'That's pretty much the gist of it.'

'This is just like something from a movie, Shae. What are you going to do?'

I shrugged. I needed time to process it all before I spoke to my parents. I wanted to see for myself the woman who had the affair with my dad all those years ago.

'I told Stella I'd call her so we could meet up again soon,' I said. For some reason I liked the idea of seeing her again, but I didn't admit that to Lexi.

I looked up my mobile for the number I had waited so desperately to hear from. My sister's phone number. I added her to my contacts. *Stella.*

Just then Dad's name flashed on the screen. I panicked as though he was at the front door, not on the phone. I'd been waiting for him to ring and today of all days, he finally rings.

'Hi, Dad,' I said, too brightly even for my ears.

'Hello, sweetheart, how are you?'

'I'm fine.'

'I'm sorry I haven't rung as often I as I should. Your mum mentioned you were a bit upset with us.'

'It doesn't matter. I'm fine about it now. Umm, I'm just about to head out with Lexi,' I lied.

'Okay, well I wanted to let you know that we're coming up on the weekend,' he said.

'Why? Are you taking me home?' I tried the still the tremble in my fingers by flicking them about.

'Not exactly. We have something we want to talk to you about.'

Don't tell me they finally want to come clean about everything with me? Especially now after I've just managed to put it all together. Well, Mum and Dad, it's a bit late for that.

I had been searching for answers, but now I wasn't sure I wanted to hear the truth from them. Especially not after today's revelations.

'Which day, because Lexi and I have tickets to see a show Saturday and she's really looking forward to it. I can't ditch her.' I couldn't believe how easily the lies formed on my lips. They practically dripped off my tongue.

'We can make it Sunday instead.'

That was three days away. Still enough time to do more snooping. The pause stretched out between the phone lines. I was tempted to ask him about Stella and confess to him that I knew about Karen.

'Shae!' Dad yelled in the receiver as I was about to hang up.

'Yeah?'

'I love you. I want you to always remember that, no matter what.' His voice was strained.

A lump in my throat swelled. I hung up knowing exactly what they wanted to talk to me about. I wrapped my arms around my waist and bent over as my stomach flip flopped about. Time had run out as far as Karen was concerned. She had set a deadline and it had expired. It wasn't my mother she wanted him to confess to, it was me. She wanted me to know about Stella and she wanted Stella's father in her life. But after all these years, why now?

Chapter 29

Thump! Thump! Thump! The banging on the wall woke me from my sleep.

'Aww,' I groaned. I was having a nice dream and wanted to go back to that happy, cosy place.

'Wake up, everyone up!' Uncle Kevin yelled.

I scratched the sleep dust from my eyes and rolled out of bed. Lexi squinted down the hallway at me.

'What are you doing, Dad?' she asked, annoyed.

'Today's the day,' said Uncle Kevin, opening Blake's door. 'Rise and shine, Mister University.'

That's when I understood what was happening. The first-round offers were emailed out today.

'Come on, Blake, it's your date with destiny,' called out Aunty Liz.

'I forgot they do this special breakfast thing,' Lexi muttered.

She plodded down the hall to the kitchen. Her hair was matted and out of place for a change. I leant in the doorway of Blake's room. He was hidden deep beneath the bed cover.

I walked over and shook the mound. There were grumblings from within and then a head popped out. He grabbed a singlet from the floor and pulled it over his head.

'Are you ready for this?' I asked.

'Ready as I'll ever be.' He shoved his cap on.

I wouldn't have suspect there was a problem if he hadn't told me. Hopefully he was exaggerating and was worried about nothing. My parents would be furious if I didn't get into university because of bad grades. Not that there was much chance of that with the close tabs they kept on my progress. Mum was a straight A student and she expected nothing less from her daughter.

I shuffled into the kitchen to find the others all seated around the table. The local newspaper sat folded in the middle with the heading printed in bold across the top. *Nervous wait over — University offers today!* I slipped into a seat and gripped my necklace. Maybe its strength could help Blake today. Blake appeared relaxed, and enjoying the fuss, although he wouldn't admit it. He's always liked being the centre of attention, especially when we were younger. Dale wasn't much better. Blake was always trying to keep up with him.

I tried to get Blake's attention, but he wouldn't look at me. Lexi wrung her hands, waiting. She was probably just as nervous as Blake. This time next year it would be our turn. That was so weird to think about. Only one more year of high school and we were done.

'Here you go, son,' said Uncle Kevin, passing a laptop across.

'Why can't he just get a text message and tell us when we wake up at a reasonable hour?' complained Lexi. 'Why do you insist on waking us all up?'

Blake grabbed the computer and took his time turning it on. The device whirred to life as the sound echoed through the kitchen.

Blake clicked on some keys. 'Want me to check if there's any sunglasses sales, Lexi?'

'Just get to your stupid emails so I can go back to bed,' she said.

'Yes, hurry up and check. Some of us have been waiting a *really* long time for this,' said Aunty Liz.

Blake clicked a couple more times, a deep breath the only tell-tale sign of nerves.

'Are you ready my baby boy?' Aunty Liz ruffled his hair.

He ducked to avoid her, but she pulled him close and kissed the top of his head.

'We are so proud of you,' she whispered.

'Mum, don't start blubbering yet, geez,' teased Lexi.

'I'm not crying,' she said, patting her eyes.

Blake cleared his throat and angled forward. 'Holy shit!'

'Blake, watch your language,' said Aunty Liz.

'I got in!' He jumped up from the table. 'I got in!'

His family crowded around to hug him. He looked across the table and I clapped my hands loudly. I couldn't believe he had doubted himself.

'Come on, read it out,' said Lexi.

They gave him some space. He cleared his throat and took the stage.

'It reads 'Blake Allery, Bachelor of Physiotherapy, James Cook University'.'

'James Cook? If you're staying in town, does that mean we don't get rid of you?' said Uncle Kevin.

'Not for at least another four years.' Blake grinned.

'I thought you couldn't wait to get out of this place,' said Lexi.

'Turns out it's not so bad around here. I've got a job, friends, free board. Why would I go anywhere else?'

'That's great news, congratulations.' I hugged Blake.

'Thanks for not saying anything,' he whispered.

'Who wants pancakes?' Aunty Liz beat some eggs into a bowl.

Uncle Kevin jumped up and flicked the kettle on and Lexi pulled the juice from the fridge.

'So, should I tell you now or later I've changed my mind about going to Uni?' said Blake.

Everything froze. It was as though somebody pressed pause on the movie screen.

'Mum. Dad. I want to defer,' said Blake.

Aunty Liz cleared her throat. 'Blake, deferring can be hard to return from.'

'Gotcha!'

Uncle Kevin rolled up the paper and whacked Blake over the head with it.

'I've heard the first year at Uni is like you've deferred anyway. You don't have to do that much work,' said Blake.

'That can't be true,' said Aunty Liz.

'It might be true for those who live on campus. Don't they party every night?' said Uncle Kevin.

'Oohh, speaking of parties. Can we still have our pool party?' Lexi asked.

Uncle Kevin's eyes narrowed. 'I thought it was for you and your friends to celebrate, Blake?'

'Yeah, it is, but Lexi has to invite some girls. It wouldn't be much of a party with just my mates sitting round.'

'If the police are called, you'll both be grounded for the rest of the holidays,' warned Aunty Liz.

'Mum, don't be ridiculous,' said Lexi. 'Besides we're too old to get grounded anymore.'

'I'm just warning you.' She continued to mix the pancake batter as the frypan sizzled.

'It'll be fine, I'll make sure of it,' said Blake. 'Now where are those pancakes?'

The front door slammed. 'Did I hear someone say pancakes?' Dale, my oldest cousin, appeared in the kitchen. He was a younger version of my uncle.

Lexi squealed. 'What are you doing home?'

He staggered backwards from her hug. 'I missed you too little sis.'

Aunty Liz's pancake flipper was poised mid-air.

'Hi, Mum,' Dale said, kissing her cheek.

She remained stunned.

'Maybe we should have told her, Dad. She could be having a heart attack,' said Dale.

Aunty Liz glared at Uncle Kevin. 'You knew about this? Why didn't you tell me?'

'That wouldn't have been nearly as much fun as seeing the look on your face right now,' he replied.

She reached across and swatted him with the flipper. With the whole family together, besides Aileen, the breakfast celebration could officially begin.

Chapter 30

Dale joined us near the kitchen table.

'So, what brings you home to Townsville?' I asked Dale. He lived three hours north at Mission Beach.

'I came home because I wanted to remind Blake who the favourite son was. Make sure he knew how happy Mum was to see me.'

'You're only the favourite son when you're here. Otherwise, it's all me.' Blake gripped Dale's hand before pulling him in for a hug.

'Where'd you get in?' asked Dale.

'James Cook, with physio,' said Blake, chest pushed out.

'I knew you wouldn't move out of home. Mumma's boy,' Dale teased.

The two boys wrestled around the kitchen.

'Hey, cut it out!' Aunty Liz yelled. 'Now sit down and eat up.'

Her smirk suggested she didn't really mind them mucking around. She brought a fresh stack of pancakes to the table.

I squeezed some lemon juice, sprinkled on some sugar, then shoved it in. 'Mmm, delicious.'

My auntie's pancakes were one of her trademark specialties. Dale rolled his pancake up and bit off half of it. 'Mmm, these are worth the drive home.'

'Maybe you should visit more often,' said Lexi.

'We'll be happy with any visits,' said Aunty Liz.

'So, how do you feel about being Grandma and Grandpa?' Dale asked. 'Or is it Nanny and Gramps?'

Silence settled in the room.

'Aren't we talking about Aileen's *situation*?' Dale asked.

Uncle Kevin cleared his throat. 'We are. It's just been a bit to get our heads around.'

'Mum, it's a baby, not the end of the world,' said Dale.

'I know that,' she snapped. 'It's just, well it's Aileen. She's always been so responsible.'

'True. We wouldn't have been surprised if it was Lexi,' Dale teased.

'Hey, watch it! That offends me,' said Lexi, smiling.

'Don't joke like that, Dale,' said Uncle Kevin. 'Your mother and I will support Aileen and we expect you all to do the same.'

'We're flying over to see her,' said Aunty Liz.

'When? How?' asked Lexi. 'Is Aileen staying there to have the baby?'

'Actually, Shae's parents are paying for the flights,' said Uncle Kevin.

All faces turned to me.

I shrugged. 'They didn't tell me.'

'We want to meet Christian and his family. Especially now they're going to be part of our family,' said Aunty Liz.

'Daniel and Susannah have kindly offered to pay for the flights,' Uncle Kevin said. 'And we've agreed, as long as they let us pay them back.'

The safe full of money flashed in my mind. There was too much money inside just to pay for flights.

'When are you going?' asked Blake.

'First, we'll wait until everyone's had time to let the news sink in. His parents are probably just as surprised as us about the whole thing. Plus, it will give Aileen and Christian a chance to talk about what they want to do.'

'You still didn't answer me,' said Dale.

'Answer what?' said Aunty Liz.

'Is it Nanna or Grandma?'

She grinned. 'Probably Nanna.'

***

After breakfast Dale, Blake and Uncle Kevin went out for a round of golf. Some 'bonding time' Uncle Kevin called it. Dale was only home for the night, then he had to go back to work. Lexi had gone with her mum to get some supplies for the party tonight.

While they were all out, I finished hanging out the washing. A deep, droning tone floated through the air. I moved closer to the fence, hoping to catch the words sung by Mr. Sampson. His voice was gravelly and weathered.

> *'Of old and new*
> *I want to do*
> *The best by you*
> *I love you true.'*

I poked my head over the fence. 'Hi, Mr. Sampson.'

He looked up, surprised. 'Hello, Shae.'

It was my turn to be caught off guard. 'How did you know my name?'

'Callen's mentioned you once or twice. He's a good boy. Parents are a bit hard on him sometimes, but they mean well.'

'That's a good thing, I guess.'

'The only bad thing with Callen is he doesn't visit me enough.' Mr. Sampson grinned.

'That song you were singing, where's it from?' I asked.

'It's from my heart.' He removed the gardening gloves and fanned himself with them.

169

'You made it up?'

He nodded. 'Sang it just before I proposed to my wife Sally.'

'Really? She must have thought you were romantic,' I said.

'She said yes, so perhaps she did think me a romantic chap.'

Mr. Sampson's back door slammed shut and Callen strolled toward us. 'You're not telling stories are you, Pop?'

'Just telling your lady friend here about Sally's song.'

I blushed at his reference to me.

'As long as you're not telling stories about me,' Callen said.

'We haven't been talking long enough for me to get around to them!'

'It's getting hot out here,' said Callen. 'Why don't you go in and sit down for a while. You've been weeding all morning.'

'That's probably a good idea. But if you want to get rid of me to talk to Shae, you could just say that.' Mr. Sampson winked at me.

'It was nice talking to you, Mr. Sampson,' I said.

'Jim. Call me Jim. It makes me feel younger,' he said, reaching for my hand.

'It was nice talking to you, *Jim.*'

'Come over and we'll talk longer next time,' he said. 'I can tell you some stories about our boy, Callen.'

I laughed as Callen shook his head. Jim made his way slowly to the back door.

'He likes you, I can tell,' said Callen.

'He said you don't visit enough,' I said.

'I thought you didn't talk about me.'

I shrugged. 'Your name might have come up.'

Callen kicked the ground. 'Don't believe everything he tells you.'

'Hey, I was wondering… Blake and Lexi are throwing a party tonight. It's kind of a celebration for Blake getting into Uni, and Lexi told me to invite you.'

He crossed his arms. 'But *you're* not inviting me?'

'Yeah, I mean, no. Why do you always confuse me?'

'It's not my fault you're easily confused,' he teased.

'You can be really annoying sometimes.'

'Why don't you just say what you mean then?' His face turned serious and he stepped closer toward the fence.

I took a deep breath. 'If you want to, I'd like it if you came to the party tonight.'

Callen took another step closer. Standing on the ledge of the fence I was taller for a change. I wanted to look away, but my eyes were drawn to his.

'I'd like that,' he said.

'Callen!' Mr. Sampson yelled through the back door. 'Your folks are here.'

Callen frowned and his shoulders became rigid. 'I'll be there in a minute.'

'Your parents are visiting? That's nice, right?' I asked.

'Depends on your definition of nice.'

'So, not nice?' I asked.

'Not awful,' he conceded.

'And you think I'm confusing!'

He laughed then shoved his hands into his pockets. 'We're sorting through some things at the moment.'

I understood exactly what he meant. It was how I felt about my parents visiting this weekend. *'We have something we want to talk to you about.'* The anticipation made my stomach churn. Would they tell me everything I wanted to know?

Chapter 31

Music pumped through the backyard as people arrived. Grub, Blake and Dale had set up some multi-coloured disco lights. Grub's cousin owned a mobile party business and he had managed to borrow them for tonight. Lexi and I then spent the afternoon arranging lanterns around the side of the pool. They hung from the bamboo poles that we had hammered into the ground. We also set up some solar flashing star lights to twinkle from the trees. All that work nearly kept my mind off my parents upcoming visit and the discovery of my sister. Nearly, but not quite.

I shook the thought of Stella away, determined not to let the questions I had about her ruin my night. Lexi and Blake had gone to a lot of trouble to have this party. The last thing I wanted was to be a party pooper and make them worry about me.

I juggled a bowl of cheese rings, a bottle of soft-drink and two packets of chicken chips as I tried to slide the back door open.

'Do you want a hand?' Simon appeared.

Without waiting for a reply he slid the door open and grabbed the drink and bowl. The backyard was filling up fast. I didn't recognise many people, but most of the guests knew each other from school. I dropped the packets of chips onto the table and Simon did the same with his load.

'It looks good.' He gestured toward the party.

'Blake and Lexi don't do things in halves, especially Lexi. Once she gets an idea in her head, there's no stopping her.'

Simon chugged down some of his drink. 'You want a beer?'

'She doesn't want a beer,' said Mikayla, bumping her hip against me and knocking me into the table. 'She wants something sweet and yummy.'

'I'll catch you later,' Simon said. 'There's something I was going to ask, but it can wait.'

'Simon's a bit cute.' Mikayla giggled.

'What happened to Brendan?'

'Brendan, shmendan, he's an idiot.' She threw her arms around me.

'How much have you had to drink already?' I asked.

She waved my question away. 'Blake told me to keep an eye on you.' Mikayla steered me toward the party. 'But don't worry, I'm not very good at doing what I'm told.'

'Good, because I don't need *another* babysitter.'

Mikayla laughed. 'Here, I've got better stuff to drink than beer.'

She handed me a cup with bubbles of pink liquid inside. I sniffed it and the bubbles zinged inside my nostrils.

'Smells nice, but no thanks, maybe later.' I handed the cup back to Mikayla. My tummy didn't feel quite right anyway. I hadn't had much appetite since meeting Stella.

Mikayla went to finish what was left inside the cup when something distracted her. I turned to see what had caught her attention. Callen walked across the yard toward me. I tried not to notice how his t-shirt fit snug across his chest. His hair flopped across one eye and he pushed it back. He didn't get far before Lexi intercepted and she pulled him in for a hug.

'What the hell is he doing here?' Kai joined us.

'He's our neighbour and it's our party, so leave him alone,' I said.

Kai slunk off to join his mates. Callen watched Kai for a moment, then his focus settled back on me. He strolled my way, hands shoved in his cargo shorts pockets.

'Hope you're planning on behaving yourself,' I said.

He leant his head to one side and smirked. 'I'll try my best.'

'Hi, I'm Mikayla.' She shoved her hand in his face.

I could see why she and Lexi were such good friends. Subtlety was not their strongest trait. He shook her hand good naturedly.

'So, you're the *neighbour* I've heard about.' She pointed her finger at him.

'Don't believe everything you hear,' he said.

I knew he was remembering our talk about those rumours.

She drained her cup. 'I'm off for a refill. Can I get you something, Callen?'

He shook his head.

'She didn't mean anything by that,' I said, apologetically.

An awkwardness lingered between us. Callen was great during the car ride home yesterday. He let me have the quiet I needed to process the fact I had just met my sister for the first time.

'Hey, thanks again for everything with Stella,' I said. 'You must think my family has the biggest issues. I swear we were normal once.'

'I think it would be weird if your family was normal. Nobody's family is perfect.' His voice became bitter. 'So, how do you feel after … yesterday?'

'I'm not sure. Weird, confused, hurt, excited. It's kind of hard to explain because my feelings seem to change every time I think about it.' I sighed. 'So, I'm trying not to think about it tonight.'

'Got it.' Callen made a zipping motion across his lips. 'No more questions.'

'Everything okay here, Shae?' Blake appeared beside me, sizing Callen up.

Callen offered his hand first. It was like a first date that I had to get approval for. Blake was cautious but polite. Before long they managed to get on to the topic of rugby. Dale joined them and they talked about games and players which was when I tuned out.

'I'll leave you boys to it.' I retreated from the rugby conversation.

A familiar face wandered into the yard. 'Hi, Shae.'

'Olly!' I crushed him with a hug.

'Whoah. I wasn't expecting that kind of reception,' he said.

'I'm glad you're here.'

'I nearly didn't come. I wasn't sure if you really wanted me to.'

'Don't be silly,' I said. 'Of course I wanted you to come. That's why I invited you.'

'Look, Shae, about the other day—'

'Forget it, I'm glad you told me. It's just …' I took a deep breath. 'My parents have been a bit weird lately and … I'm trying not to overthink it. But the more I try not to worry, the more I do.' As soon as the words left my mouth my insides coiled about, tight and aching. I took a shaky breath, hoping the feeling would pass.

'I'm sure it's nothing, Shae. Maybe they've a big surprise planned for you before we go back to school.'

I forced a smile. 'Yeah, maybe.'

Lexi appeared between us. 'Hi, Oliver.

'And I'm Mikayla.' She bumped into Lexi. 'Here, Shae. You said later … well, it's later.'

Mikayla passed me a full cup of champagne then wandered off. Lexi raised her eyebrow.

'What? I'm not planning on drinking it.'

As if she's one to judge about drinking, especially after the day at the waterfall. I poured the drink on the grass, checking around to make sure Mikayla didn't see.

'I didn't say anything …' Lexi's voice trailed off.

I followed her line of sight. A slim girl with a dangerously short skirt hugged Blake, then Dale.

'What's Nadine doing here?' said Lexi, scowling.

I shrugged. 'Blake must have invited her. This must be the date he talked about.'

'Even if he did invite her, I can't believe she'd actually turn up.'

'Lexi! Give the girl a break,' I said.

She managed to look sheepish when she realised Oliver was listening.

'Shae told me you dance,' Oliver changed topics. 'Said you're the best in Townsville.'

Lexi blushed from the compliment. Lexi blushing? That was a first.

'Shae is known to exaggerate,' said Lexi, deflecting the comment.

'Maybe you can show me later and I'll decide for myself.'

'Sounds like a challenge,' she flirted, back to her normal mode.

Maybe Oliver could take her mind off that idiot boyfriend of hers. I looked toward the pool just as Grub bombed his way into the middle of it. He emerged to cheers and whistles of adulation. He would have expected nothing less. A couple more guys followed after him and soon there were several people in the pool.

'Hey, Shae.' Simon stood off to the side, under the palm tree.

The solar lights lit up around the trunk as they flashed different colours.

I wandered over. 'What are you doing over here all alone?'

Something was off, except I couldn't work out what. He offered me his beer again, but I declined. He chugged it, then crunched the can flat.

'I was thinking, maybe we could go to the movies,' he said.

'Sure. I can check what night Lexi has off,' I said.

'I kind of meant … just you and me,' he said, reaching for my hand.

I panicked. He must have seen it in my face and quickly let go.

'Or we could see if the others want to come.' He stepped back to create space between us.

'Simon, I like you but … I'm sorry if …' The words weren't coming out the way I wanted them to.

'Don't worry about it. I must have read the signals wrong. Guess I just hoped.'

Guilt weighed down on me. 'I do like you but as a friend. I'm sorry that sounds so cliché'.' I couldn't believe I was having the *just friends* talk.

'Sure, the friend thing is good.' Simon forced a smile. 'So, do friends get a hug?'

I smiled. 'I think they do.'

He squeezed tight. 'He's a lucky guy,' he whispered, then let me go.

I watched him join the party again, confused by his comment. Through the crowd Callen was watching. Our eyes met and I couldn't help but look away first. I hadn't done anything wrong, yet it felt like I had. Great! Now I was feeling guilty about two guys and neither one was even my boyfriend.

Chapter 32

I searched the crowd as Lexi casually dropped her hand onto Oliver's arm and threw her head back with laughter. Her blonde hair cascaded down her back and she genuinely looked like she was enjoying herself with Olly. I hoped Kai wasn't anywhere nearby to witness her flirtations. In the back corner, Mikayla was bent over some bushes. Her denim skirt rode up at the back.

'Mikayla! You're nearly flashing your knickers,' I said, tugging on her skirt.

'Shae!' She stood up and threw her arms around me, losing her balance. 'Don't worry, I got my shexy new shilky ones on tonight,' she slurred.

I tried to steady her, but my balance shifted. 'Are you okay?'

'I'm great.' She looked around. 'Cool party.'

'How much have you had to drink?' I asked.

'Not that much, so here you go.' She passed the full glass to me. 'Pour that down the hatch.'

I took the glass, but didn't drink any of it.

'Come on, just a little, bitty, itshy drink for me,' said Mikayla.

'Umm, I think you've had enough.'

Mikayla burped. 'Nope, I think I'll have some more.'

I moved the glass out of her reach. 'How about we get you some water.'

Mikayla slumped to the ground, ignoring my suggestion. 'I think Simon likes you.'

'Not anymore.' I sat down beside her. 'I told him I only wanted to be friends.'

'Friends? But Simon's cute! Oohh, is there something going on with you and that Callen guy?' She tried to reach for the glass again, but the effort knocked it from my hand. 'Whoopsy!' Mikayla laughed at the mess she'd made. 'Hey, you know Callen put a guy in hospital?' Mikayla hiccupped. 'Beat him up and left him there. The guy was in a coma for days.'

'He's not like that,' I said.

'He must have been at some stage,' she said, serious. 'People like that don't usually change, Shae.'

I searched through the faces in the crowd until I saw Callen talking to some girl with cleavage spilling out her singlet.

'Looks like he's not my problem anyway,' I said.

Callen reached for the girl's hair. I looked away. I didn't need to see any more.

I couldn't believe I had invited him to the party. If I'd know he was just going to try and pick up one of the girls here, I wouldn't have bothered. I should have gone with my first instinct, and Mikayla had just confirmed it. The guy was trouble.

'I have to pee,' I said to Mikayla.

I moved through the crowd toward the back door. I needed the toilet, but that wasn't the real reason I walked away from Mikayla. Every time I thought I had things under control, something changed. Callen was so understanding about yesterday when he first arrived at the party, and then I catch him off flirting with some random girl. Things were moving too fast around me and I couldn't keep up. As

I pushed through the crowd, I decided I needed some air and space away from everyone. Just for a minute to pull myself together.

Something weird was going on with my stomach. It had started to churn like someone had put the spin cycle on. Why did I feel nauseous? Maybe it was stress. But didn't stress just give you a headache? I didn't have one of them. But the whole thing with Mum and Dad was really getting to me. Not to mention Lexi being so different this visit. I was really starting to wonder who this new Lexi was? And there was Stella. How was she going to fit in to the picture now? So much for not thinking about things tonight!

I veered off toward the side of the house and stumbled along the path. The heat rose up my neck and my head started to spin. I didn't feel well and collapsed on the steps. I held my head in my hands. A heat rushed up my neck to my forehead then away again. I tried to focus on a rock on the ground and breathe through the rising bile.

'Shae, are you okay?'

I know that voice.

I vomited up what little food I had eaten today. Another wave of nausea overcame me. I retched again, adding to the first pile. The stench made me cringe and another bout of projectile came out. I groaned and tried to breathe through my nose.

'I'll be right back.'

That voice again.

I needed air to clear my head and still the swirling stars circling the night sky. Slowly the rock I tried hard to look at before came into focus. My forehead became cold as someone held a damp face washer there. I groaned, knowing who my nurse would be.

'It'll pass in a minute. Just keep taking those deep breaths,' said Callen.

'I don't need your help,' I said pushing the cloth away. 'Why don't you go back to chatting up whatever her name was.'

Callen handed me a glass. 'Here you go, drink some water.'

I didn't want to accept it, but my mouth felt like a cotton ball.

'Must have been something I ate,' I said.

'Well, it wasn't those bubbles Mikayla was throwing back.'

'Were you spying on us?'

Callen squatted in front of me. He wiped the face washer along my forehead, then across my mouth.

'I wasn't spying, just observing,' he said. 'And for the record, I'm not chatting up anyone. There was only one girl I was interested in seeing here tonight.'

He pushed a piece of hair out of my eye and trailed a finger down my cheek. It wasn't the upset tummy giving me a fluttering feeling this time.

'What did you observe … from afar?' I asked.

'Someone looking out for a friend. Someone caring and thoughtful and kind.'

He helped me to my feet. I teetered a bit, but he kept his arm around my waist. I leaned into him as my body continued to shake from vomiting. I needed to lie down and make it stop.

'Can you take me to bed?' I asked.

'I thought you'd never ask.'

I tried to whack him, but it was only a tap. 'Not. Funny.'

He led me back to the party and toward the back door. The crowd had thickened. The music blared and the lights were bright. Callen guided me carefully through the people.

'What are you still doing here?' Kai poked Callen in the chest.

Callen's grip around me tightened. He tried to get past, but Kai's frame blocked the way.

'Hey, I'm talking to you, loser,' said Kai.

Guests stopped talking to watch the drama about to unfold.

'I asked you a question.' Kai shoved Callen in the chest.

Callen clenched his fist, but he didn't push back. 'Let it go, Kai,' he said.

Lexi appeared. 'What's going on?'

Callen moved me toward her.

'What's the matter with your girlfriend?' asked Kai. 'Too much for a loser like you, is she?'

'You should watch that mouth of yours, Kai,' said Callen. 'From memory, it's what got you into trouble last time.'

Kai stepped closer. He said something I couldn't make out, then pushed Callen again. Callen held his ground and the two become embroiled in a headlock. Kai swung wildly and a spurt of blood flew out from Callen's nose. A splatter of blood trailed across Callen's t-shirt. Then Callen punched Kai in the stomach. Kai grunted and fell to his knees.

The crowd had moved out of the way, clearing a path between the two. Kai charged Callen. They stumbled and Kai tried to get in another punch, but their bodies were too close together. They twisted and shoved. *Splash!* A cheer ran through the party as they landed in the pool. The crowd rushed forward to see what would happen next.

Callen swam to the edge and pulled himself out. Kai glared at him from the water. Blake and Dale moved in the middle on the ledge, creating a barrier between the two.

'Just stay there,' said Dale, watching Kai.

'I didn't want any trouble and I sure didn't start it,' said Callen, teeth gritted.

'I know, but you can finish it.' Blake gripped Callen's shoulder. 'He's not worth it.'

Callen took a step back. He pulled his t-shirt off and wiped his nose with it. The blood had stopped, but that black eye would be hard to hide in the morning. He looked around the party, saw me with Lexi, then left.

Chapter 33

I rode along the trail that ran parallel with the Weir. The fresh air was meant to clear my head. It was throbbing when I woke up this morning and the painkillers had only dulled it.

'Hey, I was thinking maybe we could go to the movies.' I groaned at the memory. I hoped Simon wasn't mad at me. I didn't even say good night to him. After the fight broke up, I lay down for a while, but most people had gone by the time I got up again. I made Lexi promise not to tell her parents about me being sick. I didn't want them telling my parents about it. Besides I didn't know if it was stress that caused it or just bad luck. One thing from last night was strikingly clear. There was a history between Kai and Callen that wasn't good.

The primary school passed by on the right, and a lone figure kicked a ball about. I knew the profile well. Callen was absorbed in his own world. I wasn't sure I was ready to face him just yet. He said he wasn't flirting with that girl and I wanted to believe him, but I had to be wary. He was still hiding something from me. Kai's confrontation with him last night proved that.

I was about to ride on when he looked up and waved. I dismounted and removed my helmet. I tried to fix my hair, but it couldn't be helped.

As Callen got closer, the shiner left on his face from Kai's fist became clearer. The mottled purple and black colour framed his right eye and had spread across his nose.

'Wow, I thought I looked awful,' I teased.

He pushed some hair off my face. 'You don't look so bad.'

I looked away.

'You were a bit … out of sorts last night,' he said. 'Do you know what caused it?

I shook my head. 'One minute I was trying to coax Mikayla into drinking water and the next, urrggh,' I said.

'Go easy on yourself, Shae. You've had a lot going on in your world lately. Take some time out if you need.'

I nodded. And Callen didn't even know the whole story. Not like I did.

'At least after you spewed, you seemed better,' he joked.

My eyes grew wide and I turned away from him. He didn't need to remind me that he saw me vomit.

He spun me around. 'Hey, don't worry about it. It wasn't your fault.'

I remembered Callen's gentle touch as he applied a cold washer to my forehead. Just like the night I bumped my head and he applied ice. He had shown me his caring side once again.

'Thanks for helping look after me.'

'Anytime.' He smiled a half squint with his black eye. 'Do you want to ditch your wheels, maybe walk for a bit?' he asked.

We walked for a while before we came to a lookout. It was a great view of the Gleeson Weir. You could see part of the crossing where Lexi played that stupid prank. It was so long ago already. So much had changed in between.

'I think the party finished up earlier than Blake and Lexi planned,' I said.

'Oh geez, I'm really sorry about that. I'll have to come over and apologise to them. I never meant for anything to go down between me and Kai.'

'It's fine. They don't blame you for any of it.'

He shook his head. 'It still shouldn't have happened. That's not who I am.'

I turned toward him. 'I believe you.' I reached up toward his bruised eye. Slowly, waiting for him to stop me, but he didn't. I ran my fingertips along his forehead.

He closed his eyes. 'That feels nice.'

I continued tracing around his eye, down his cheekbone and along his jawline. He grabbed my hand and moved it toward his mouth. Gently he kissed the top of it.

'Can you tell me the story between you and Kai? Please?' I asked.

He dropped my hands. 'I used to date Kai's sister. He didn't like it, so of course I kept seeing her.' He shrugged. 'He didn't think I was good enough. Guess I don't blame him.'

'Did you care about her?'

Callen leant back against the rail. 'Sondra was great. She didn't care about following the crowd like other girls. We only went out for a couple of months. But she adored her brother. Maybe that was why she believed *him* when I really needed her to believe *me*.'

'What didn't she believe?' I asked.

'What does it matter? She broke up with me because she thought I was lying and I haven't seen her since. I might do a lot of things, Shae, but I don't lie.'

I waited for him to go on, but he didn't. 'Callen, you know things about me nobody else does. My sister, my father's affair. You can trust me so just tell me the whole story, please.'

'You already know it. You've heard the rumours, remember?'

'I want to hear your story.' I put my hand over his. 'I will believe you. I promise.'

185

He squeezed his eyes tight. The purple bruising made the pain on his face raw. I could tell he was fighting with himself, deciding what to do. He turned to look out at the view. It seemed to give him the courage he needed to tell his story.

'One night something happened and I saw Kai for what he really was.' Callen's voice took on a hard edge. His fists clenched on the railing. 'The problem is that people like Kai don't want others to know what they're really like. Plus, it helps if their parents are loaded and can bail them out of trouble anytime.'

'What happened?' I asked.

'Doesn't matter, it's done. But he'll get his own back one day.'

'Callen, did it have anything to do with a guy? Did you put somebody in a coma?' I let the words tumble out because there wouldn't be another chance to ask.

'How do you know about that?'

'So, you did?'

'Do you think I would do that? Could do that?' Confusion spread across his face. Hurt.

'No.' I swallowed. 'That's not who you are.'

'It was Kai. He threw the punch that knocked the guy out. One punch, that's all it took. The guy smacked his head on the concrete. *Whack!* I'll never forget that sound. Like slapping a cold, dead fish on the table.

'At the police station it was Kai's word against mine. I already had an *incident* attached to my name from a couple of months before. It was nothing major.' He shrugged. 'I was with a couple of mates near an abandoned house and got a warning about trespassing, but who do you think they believed? Besides, Kai and his parents sweetened the deal with a little cash injection to help the guy recover. This guy needed money and he got a bonus if he recovered with the *right* memories from the night.'

'The right memories? You mean, pointing the finger at you?'

Callen nodded, jaw clenched.

'Did you know the guy?' I remembered the night we walked home from roller skating. 'Who was he?' I was sure I already knew the answer.

'It was Fish. I was out with him the night Kai ran into us. Kai was off his face on something. Started in on me about his sister. Fish told him to back off and that's when Kai swung. It caught Fish off guard and it was lights out for him. *Splat*! I hear that sound over and over at night. I thought my best mate was dead.'

'I'm confused. If he was your friend, why would he blame you?'

'Because I told him to,' explained Callen.

'What? Why would you do that?'

'Kai pointed the finger at me before Fish had given his version. The cops already thought I did it. Fish was unconscious for a couple of days so he couldn't speak up. By then Kai had everybody convinced it was me.

'I denied it at first, but the police didn't believe me. Sondra was my girlfriend and she didn't believe me. Kai had his lie so perfectly laid out that my truth didn't stand a chance against her brother. My own parents didn't even believe me!

'When Fish woke up, Kai offered him money. Fish's family really needed the money so I told him to take it. One of us might as well get something out of a crappy situation. I figured I'd only get a slap on the wrists, maybe some community service so I told Fish to back up Kai's story. Told him to say it was just one punch and he hit his head. Two mates having a disagreement that got out of control.'

I moved away to put some space between us. I wasn't expecting such a confession.

'Shae?'

I didn't answer.

Callen blocked my path. 'Do you believe me?'

I inhaled the sweet smell of him, overpowering my senses and thoughts. I didn't understand how he could take the blame for something he didn't do.

'Shae, do you believe me?' he repeated.

'Yes,' I whispered, my body tight with tension.

He pulled me in and held me tight. 'Thank you.'

I wrapped my arms around him. His heart pounded through the cotton of his t-shirt. It matched mine beat for beat.

'Shae?'

I reluctantly loosened my grip and looked up.

'There's something I've wanted to do for a while,' he said.

His hands cupped both sides of my face. His lips moved forward.

'Is this, okay?' he asked.

I nodded and moved closer to him. My breath hitched as his mouth covered mine. He kissed me again, longer this time. My head spun and I didn't want him to stop, but he did. I looked up and discovered two boys watching us.

'We'll have to finish this another time,' Callen whispered in my ear.

'Sam? Charlie? There you are.' A flustered mother came round the corner.

'They were kissing',' the taller one said.

'Boys, let's go.' She grabbed their hands and dragged them away.

'Do they love each other?' the shorter one asked.

I buried my face in Callen's shoulder as it shook with silent laughter. Our first kiss came with an audience. Nothing was ever straight forward.

Chapter 34

As Callen pushed my bike toward home, the warm breeze blew my hair about my face. I pulled it back with a hair band.

'I like it out,' said Callen.

'Really? It looks like my parents must be poodles.'

He laughed. 'It looks like spiral pasta, my favourite kind.'

'More like fairy floss, fluffy and messy,' I said.

Callen grinned and reached for my hand. I let him take it.

'There's something I don't understand,' I said. It had been bugging me since Callen's confession.

His grip tightened, but he didn't let go.

'Why does Kai hate you so much if he's the one in the wrong?'

'That's why he hates me,' said Callen. 'I've got a secret over him like nobody else. Not even Fish.'

'I thought Fish knew you didn't really hit him.'

'When he woke up, he couldn't remember anything. He didn't think I hit him, but that's what he'd been told. It stung that even for a minute he believed I would do that to him. We'd been mates for so long, he should have known I'd never do that. He swore he knew all along it was Kai, but I'm not so sure he did. Or maybe I was just mad at the whole damn world after that night. I know it was hard for Fish to let me take the blame and I haven't really made it easy for him. We haven't been the same kind of friends since.'

'You miss him, don't you?'

'Yeah. But it works both ways. He could contact me if he wanted to.'

'You can only push people away so many times before they stop coming back,' I said. 'He did reach out the other night. Are you going to call him?'

'Maybe. I dunno.'

We paused outside as the curtain in Mr. Sampson's house moved.

'Think we've got another audience,' I said, flicking my head toward the house.

'Pop likes to keep an eye out for me. He tells me I'm too quick to judge my parents.'

'Are you?' I asked.

'Probably.' He shrugged. 'Now we're still on tomorrow, right? Magnetic Island?'

'Yeah, of course.' I was secretly counting down to spending the whole day alone with Callen.

'Good, because I've got a surprise for you.' He walked up the driveway as the curtain moved back into place again.

My phone rang. 'Hello?'

'Shae? Hi, it's Stella.'

'Stella, hi,' I said.

The silence stretched out.

'I was wondering if maybe … well I hoped we could … can I see you?' Stella asked.

'Umm sure. When?'

'You don't seem very busy now.'

'How do you know I'm not busy?' I turned around as Stella waved to me from a car across the road. I waited for the traffic to clear before crossing the road. 'What are you doing here?' I asked.

'Please don't get mad or think I'm stalking you again,' said Stella. 'It's just, I knew where you were staying and I've been thinking about you since the sanctuary. When I pulled up, I saw you talking to your *bodyguard*.'

'Stella!'

'I know I'm rambling, I'm sorry. I do that when I'm nervous, I can't help it. I wanted to see you again. Maybe hang out for a bit, but only if you want to.' The apprehension was clear on her face.

I nodded. 'I want to.'

She jerked her head toward the passenger seat. 'What are you waiting for then? Jump in.'

I rushed around to the passenger side and climbed inside my sister's car. My sister. That was going to take some getting used to.

***

Stella parked out the front of the Townsville Botanical Gardens.

'I want to show you something,' she said.

I followed her along a straight path until we came to a huge fountain. A bungee trampoline sat on the grass nearby. Stella turned onto a smaller pathway and slowed her pace.

'Mum used to bring me here. It was my favourite place to visit when I was younger.'

We entered the frangipani lawn section and were surrounded by a selection of the most beautiful flowers. Stella gently caressed one with a yellow centre. The edges looked as though they had been dipped in a bright magenta ink. She bent down and inhaled.

'Try it,' she said.

I breathed in the sweet, fruit aroma.

'When I was a little girl, I would move from one plant to another touching and smelling each one. Mum once told me that

191

the frangipani was a symbol of love. She said that some people use them in love spells. Do you believe in magic and spells?'

I shrugged. 'I haven't really thought about it.'

'Here, just in case.' She pulled a small hair clip with a purple frangipani on the end from her hair and pushed it into the side of my hair.

'Is there a spell on this one?' I asked.

'I don't think you need a love spell. It looked to me like it might have already found you.'

I laughed. 'It's kind of new. I don't really know what it is yet.'

I couldn't explain to Stella how complicated it was with Callen. Our situation was messy enough!

'Thanks for coming here with me,' said Stella. 'It means a lot. I've never had much in the way of family.'

'Has it always been just you and Karen?'

Stella nodded. 'Mum left home as soon as she could, way before she had me. We haven't seen any of her family in years.'

I couldn't imagine not seeing my cousins, but being an only child, I understood well.

'She never spoke about my dad, even when I asked her. I used to imagine he was off saving the world, like a Greenpeace crusader you know. Saving the world one animal at a time. That was easier to accept than the fact he didn't want to know about me.'

'Is that what she told you?' I asked.

Stella shook her head. 'It's what I used to think when I cried myself to sleep at night wondering where he was.'

I suddenly understood that it wasn't just my world that had been turned upside down. I pulled Stella in for a hug and she squeezed me tight.

'Come on, I've got an idea.' She led me back the way we came.

My stomach sank. I knew where she was taking me.

'Hello, Stella!' The bungee trampoline operator waved.

'Hi, Mark, how's business today?'

He nodded. 'Can't complain.'

'No one cares anyway,' they said together and laughed.

Stella pulled me forward. 'This is my sis … this is Shae.'

'You girls want a turn? Jump on,' he said.

I backed away. 'Oh no, there's no way I can jump high.'

'Don't be a baby, come on.' Stella dragged me over and put the harness on.

'You don't have to go high, just jump.' She clipped herself into the other harness.

I watched her then did the same. Then I gripped the cables and tried not to move.

'Are you ready, Shae?' Stella started jumping and soon spun around, squealing with pleasure.

I pushed against the trampoline. Not high at first.

'Jump harder, Shae. Let go, you'll love it,' said Stella. 'Yeeew!'

My feet took on a life of their own. They pushed harder and my body moved higher and higher. Before long I was flying through the air.

'Spin around,' yelled Stella. 'Let go!'

I pushed as hard as I could. Like the somersault into the pool, my body spun. I screamed with fear, delight and surprise exhilaration. Then just like that, I let go of my fear and embraced the moment. And it felt amazing.

Chapter 35

The next day the passenger ferry docked along the jetty off the shore of Magnetic Island. There was a bottleneck as we disembarked and everyone left from the single line exit. I tried to ignore the closeness of Callen behind me.

'I can't believe you've never been to Magnetic Island.' His voice was soft in my ear.

'You better make a good tour guide,' I said.

We emerged from the narrow corridor and walked along the jetty. The heat stung my skin. I rustled through my beach bag for the sunglasses conveniently borrowed from Lexi's collection. She shouldn't care that I borrowed them. She probably wouldn't even notice they were missing. I popped them on and looked toward the water. I imagined the cool sensation if I were to dive in. It gave me a shiver. We strolled along the pier until we reached the mainland.

'My grandparents would bring me here when I was a kid,' said Callen. 'They used to rent a Mini Moke and we would cruise around the island.'

'What's a Mini Moke?' I asked. 'Like a tandem bike or something?'

'Not quite, but it is the best way to get around this island.' He winked. 'Wait here.'

I studied the information board as he disappeared. There was a tourist map, but it looked like it would be hard to get lost. The road only covered part of the island anyway. The other half was inaccessible with bushland. The signboard told the history of Magnetic Island. The traditional Aboriginal land owners, the Wulgurukaba people, called it *Yunbenun*. It was renamed by Captain James Cook who was convinced the island messed with the compass of his ship, *The Endeavour*, like a magnet.

A high-pitched horn blared and interrupted my history lesson. Callen hung out from a windowless vehicle. 'Let's go!' He banged the top of the roof like a drum.

'You're not serious?'

There were no doors, or walls and only a bar that ran along the side of the seats to grip onto. It looked like a sand buggy.

'This is a Mini Moke. It belongs to a mate who lives on the island. Well, he doesn't live here anymore, but his parents still do.'

I threw my backpack on the floor and climbed inside. Callen jammed a cap on my head.

'Don't look so worried. Just hold tight,' he said.

I gripped the bar as Callen fumbled with the clutch, making the vehicle hop forward.

'Want me to drive?' I asked

'The gears are a little closer than I'm used to is all,' he said. 'Here we go.'

With a rev it took off. The wind whipped around inside. Now I understood the hat.

'Where are we going?' I yelled over the noise of the car.

'Nelly Bay. It's not too far.'

He honked the horn as I took in the view. You could see the Townsville coastline from here. It looked a lot further than eight kilometres to shore.

A couple of years ago we sat on the Strand and watched competitors swim from the island to shore. It was the first year they made the swim cage-less so the swimmers were surrounded by kayakers, surf ski paddlers and other support boats in case they got into trouble.

The car engine strained, then slowed down as we pulled into Nelly Bay.

'Ever been snorkelling?' Callen asked.

I shook my head.

Callen rubbed his hands together. 'This is going to be great. You'll love it.' He retrieved a bag from behind the back seat.

We made our way to the deserted beach and he dumped the bag on the sand. Snorkelling equipment spilt out. There was enough for the both of us.

'You can swim right?' he asked.

I whacked him with a flipper.

'Just checking, because I've seen the way you dive.'

'Ha, very funny.'

'This is an easy snorkel. There's a harder one around further at Geoffrey Bay.' He passed me a mask. 'Come on, we'll try some breathing in the shallows.'

I hesitated.

'What's wrong?'

I glanced at my backpack, worried about what was in the front pocket.

'Shae?'

I bent down and retrieved the gold bracelet. I read the inscription *Sondra*, and scrunched up my hand. I hoped I didn't ruin the day before it began. 'Don't get mad, but I think this belongs to you, or at least, was important to you.'

I dropped the bracelet onto his palm and recognition lit up his face.

'I didn't put it together until you told me about Sondra. It was hers, wasn't it?'

He nodded. 'She threw it at me the day she dumped me. When she believed Kai's lies.'

He scrunched his fist tight.

'Callen, you have to make a choice. Hang on to your anger at Sondra. Or let it go. It can't be both.' I shook my head. 'That will only eat you up inside.'

Callen took a deep breath then stormed toward the bin near the parked car. He flung the bracelet inside and stood stiff for a moment, hands on hips. After a minute he returned to me.

'That's called letting go.' He smiled. 'Come on, let's go find some treasures.'

He removed his singlet. I tried not to stare at his bare chest, but it was hard not to. I slipped out of my clothes and was suddenly self-conscious. He had already seen me in a bikini, but we weren't alone that day.

I picked up my snorkelling gear and followed him down to the water. It was warm in the shallows. We moved out further, away from the shoreline. It was sheltered in the bay making the water calm. Callen explained how to breathe underwater. He adjusted my mask and repeated the process to fit his own. Then he stuck his head under the water. I tried to copy him, but as soon as I put my head under, I panicked and came back up for air.

'Just take your time. There's no rush,' he said.

I tried again until I was more comfortable breathing with the snorkel. Callen gave me a thumbs up underwater when I managed to stay down longer than three seconds. We came up at the same time.

Callen put his hand on my chest. 'It's all in your breathing. In slowly, then release.'

My skin burned where his fingers sat, but I followed his directions. In slowly, then release. In slowly, release.

'Good, that's really good, Shae. Next up, flippers.'

The rubber cut into my feet, but I managed to squeeze them on. I tried to flip my feet up and down.

'They're weird at first, but you'll get used to them. Make sure you bend your knees as well. Don't just rely on flicking your ankles,' said Callen.

I rolled onto my back and practiced. It was easy to float and be propelled backwards. I rolled over and tried it face down. After a while I got the hang of it both ways.

'Let's do this,' I said, popping up from the water.

I was ready to explore the underwater world. At least that's what I told myself as I spat out salt water. I was afraid, but it was a good fear, an excited anticipation. Callen wiped a loose strand of hair away from my face. His hair sat flat and I could take in his whole face. Dark eyes watched me with soft lips that had kissed me.

'Do you trust me?' he asked.

Were we still talking about snorkelling? I nodded because either way, I did.

Chapter 36

We paddled out toward the bobbing surface floats. Callen stayed by my side the whole way. Once we reached the first float, I rested against it, puffed.

I pulled the mask off. 'I never knew snorkelling was such hard work.'

'These floats are the guide for the snorkel trail. If you come up and feel disoriented just head to one of these,' Callen explained

I followed the trail that went on for about a hundred metres. I looked back toward the shore. Our bags were just a speck on the sand. Even when I went boogie boarding, I'd never been out this far to catch the waves.

'If you start to panic underwater, just look for the light. It will always be up so just swim toward it.'

I was comforted by his confidence. 'How do you know so much about snorkelling?'

'Seth, the Mini Moke owner, taught me,' explained Callen. 'We'd spend whole weekends out here.'

'Where is he now?'

Callen frowned. 'He joined the navy. Loved snorkelling that much he decided a water life was for him.'

'You say that like it's a bad thing,' I said.

'Not bad, just dangerous. Eventually he wants to be a clearance diver.'

'What does that involve?'

'Stuff like retrieval operations and underwater explosions, that kind of thing.'

'You must miss him,' I said.

He nodded. 'He lets me use his things whenever I come over. I just ring his parents and they leave the car ready for me. I used to stay here all the time before he went off to the academy. His folk are like my adoptive parents. They even leave me lunch and treats if they know I'm coming. Seth is pretty close to them, so a visit from me keeps him happy as well.'

The unspoken truth of the broken relationship with his mum and dad rang out loud and clear. *My own parents didn't even believe me.*

'Come on, let's see what we can find below today.' Callen floated off, face down.

I released my grip from the safety of the surface float. I tried to concentrate on my breathing and not kick my legs too much. It was easier to move around in the deeper water. Soon I was confident to breathe and not swallow salt water. That's when I started to take in the delights of the reef. The underwater scenery was like another world, perfect and untouched. If this was just a small part of the Great Barrier Reef, I could only imagine what other parts were like. I had seen it before through a glass bottom boat in Port Douglas, but never like this. I felt like an intruder in this underwater world. The coral was amazing. It looked soft and silky, but I didn't dare touch it to find out. The pastel colours contrasted with each other. There were all shades of orange, green, purple and blue.

Some bright shimmering fish darted past. They startled me and it took a moment to get my breathing even again. Callen swam over to me and I gave him a thumbs up. I followed after him and he pointed out things on the way. We continued away from the reef and soon the water became sparse with things to look at. Callen tapped me on the shoulder and pointed upwards. We resurfaced after we had made the short distance back to the float.

'What did you think?'

I grinned. 'Are you kidding? That was amazing! No wonder you and Seth spent all your time out here.'

'Did you see the clownfish?' he asked.

The orange and white fish from the cartoon movie sprang to mind. 'Yeah, except they were smaller than I expected.'

'Did you think they would be like on the T.V?'

'No!' I splashed him. 'But that spiky looking coral was a bit creepy.'

'That's the Staghorn Coral,' he said. 'Those spikes can grow up to two metres.'

'I like the other wavy one better. Much friendlier.'

'That was probably the Lettuce Coral,' he said.

'You're like an aquatic encyclopedia,' I teased.

'Don't tell anyone. Might ruin my reputation.'

'Your secret is safe with me.'

'Did you see the bright yellow fish with the patch over their eyes? They're the butterfly fish. The butterfly fish are very loyal,' he said, becoming serious. 'Once they find a mate, they stay together for life.'

I felt like I was still underwater trying to control my breathing. Callen floated closer toward me.

'I haven't told anyone about Kai and Fish, at least not the real story' said Callen. 'Figured nobody believed me then, why would they believe me now? Then you came along.'

'I'm not going to tell anyone, if that's what you're worried about,' I assured him.

'I'm not worried, it's just, I changed for a while. Sondra didn't believe me, neither did my parents. My friendship with Fish became weird and strained. Still is.' Callen shrugged. 'I guess I felt like there was nobody I could trust anymore, until now.'

Our legs bumped together underwater. We stayed touching, connected.

'What about telling your parents the truth now?' I asked.

'What for? It doesn't matter anymore.'

'Of course, it does. Why do you think you ended up at your Pop's house?'

'I was angry about everything so *we*, that is *they*, decided I needed some space,' said Callen.

'Exactly. You were angry because your parents thought the worst. Did you ever give them a reason to think you *didn't* hit Kai?'

'Whose side are you on?' he said.

'Yours! But you have to help yourself. Just tell them the truth! I can see that lying to them is eating you up.'

'*The truth will set you free?*' he quoted.

'Maybe.'

His leg pulled me closer. 'At least the anger wasn't wasted.'

'What do you mean?' I asked.

'It's how I ended up next door and met you.'

'It's a bit ironic don't you think? Your parents needed space from you and my parents needed space from me.'

His hands rested gently on my waist. His touch was light, yet the pressure was almost too much. 'I guess we should be thanking them. Otherwise, we wouldn't have met,' said Callen, quietly.

My hand rested on his shoulder as his hands curled further around my back.

'Why else should we thank them?' I asked.

'Because, otherwise we wouldn't be here, spending this incredible day together.'

I draped my other hand around his neck. 'Any other reason we should say thanks?'

'Because otherwise … I wouldn't be able to do this.' He pulled me closer and our lips met. A kiss so gentle, yet so intense I could barely breathe. I wrapped my hands around his neck. We stayed that way. Connected. Together. Both of us whole again.

Chapter 37

Snorkelling had been the best surprise. For the first time since our cancelled holiday, I wasn't obsessing over why. In fact, I didn't even think of my parents or Karen or Stella.

On the way home I asked Callen something that had been on my mind. 'I was wondering about that community service thing. What exactly do you have to do?'

'Remember when you saw me with the bikes? Well, our crew had been fixing them up for disadvantaged kids. We took them for a test ride that day to make sure they didn't fall apart.'

'I get it. Kind of giving back something to right your wrongs?'

'I guess you could look it that way.' Callen sighed. 'Most of the people I've met from it aren't bad people. They've just made stupid choices with no support. I've been thinking about this big brother program you can sign up for. They pair you up with a young boy to hang out with. It might be good for me, but nah, it's probably a stupid idea.'

'You should do it. You'd be good at it. You could teach them about snorkelling!'

We pulled into the driveway and my feeling of serenity vanished. 'That's my parent's car. They're not supposed to be here until tomorrow.'

'We have something we want to talk to you about.'

I panicked. I wasn't ready for this conversation. Maybe I was wrong and it was something completely different they wanted to talk to me about. The knot in my stomach tightened.

'Do you want me to come in with you?' Callen asked.

I did want him by my side. I wanted him to hold my hand and tell me everything would be all right. I wanted him to reassure me that my world wasn't about to change forever. But most of all I wanted the secrets out in the open. Once I talked to my parents there was no going back because I would have the answers. But I had to face this on my own.

I shook my head. 'Thanks anyway.'

'You know Gandhi once said, *Nobody can hurt me without my permission*. That means you have to stay strong, Shae.' He held my hand. 'You are strong. You can get through this.'

I leaned across and kissed him. *Bang.* Lexi thumped on the bonnet making us both jump.

'What's the matter?' I slammed the door.

'You need to get inside, now! They've been waiting for you all day,' she said.

'They weren't meant to be here until tomorrow.'

'Well, they're here and there's something big going on. I've been kicked out of the kitchen the whole time waiting for you to get back.'

'Why didn't you call me?'

'I did! I've left a dozen messages,' Lexi said.

I dug into my bag and pulled out my phone. The screen was black. She grabbed my hand. 'Say goodbye to your *boyfriend* and let's go!'

If Callen didn't think I was messed up before, he sure would now.

'Do you think they know that I know about Karen?' I asked.

'I think you're about to find out. The truth is coming out today, Shayzie, I just know it.'

Breathe in. Breathe out. Deep breath in. Deep breath out. As soon

205

as I entered the kitchen Dad pushed his chair out.

'Where have you been?' demanded Mum.

'What's going on? I thought you guys were coming tomorrow.' I tried to keep calm, but the tension was already thick in the room.

'That's strange because we thought you went to a show today with Lexie,' said Mum.

'I spent the day with a friend, big deal.'

My aunt and uncle looked everywhere but at me. Mum pulled a chair out and indicated for me to sit down.

'Lexi, why don't you go out the back,' Aunty Liz said.

'No!' I pulled her closer to me. 'She can stay.' It was four adults against one teenager at the moment. Lexi could help even up the sides.

'Can you at least sit down?' said Mum.

Her tone was angry, like I was the one in the wrong. As though this whole mess was somehow my fault.

I snapped. 'Why don't we just get on with whatever it is? Or perhaps I should save you both some time.'

'What are you talking about, Shae?' said Mum.

Her tone infuriated me. *How could little sheltered Shae possibly know what was going on?*

'Don't pretend that you don't know. Even I know about Karen.' Mum sank to the chair.

'I even know about Stella because I've already met my *sister*. Dad's other daughter. That's right, I know everything. I know that you've both been lying to me since I was born so let's just get this over with. Or is there something else I don't know?'

Silence.

'This is so typical. Even now, with everything I know, you're still not being honest with me. I have a right to know the whole story.'

'Daniel, tell her,' Aunty Liz said.

'Liz, stay out of it,' said Mum.

'Susannah, she knows half-truths. Bits of this and bits of that. For goodness' sake, just give her the whole story.'

Dad slammed his fist onto the kitchen bench. 'You weren't supposed to find out like this.'

'Just tell her,' Mum said, her voice breaking. 'I can't do this anymore, Daniel. Liz is right. We have to tell her the whole truth.'

Mum walked toward me and reached for my hands. 'This is really hard to say, but it's time you learnt the truth. You're not mine, Shae. I never gave birth to you.'

The air rushed from my lungs. A roaring noise built inside my head, like a jet plane flying overhead. The room spun. I tried to focus on Mum, but she had blurred into two.

'Don't you see? *Karen* is your biological mother. I was desperate to have a child. We'd already had three miscarriages. The fourth pregnancy went nearly full term. Do you have any idea what it's like to deliver a baby knowing they will never take a breath in your arms?'

'Susannah, nobody's judging you,' said Aunty Liz, softly.

'Don't try and make me feel better, Liz. You were blessed with four beautiful children with no effort at all.'

Aunty Liz flinched from the words.

'Dad?' I looked toward him. 'Dad? Tell me this isn't true.'

Bloodshot eyes looked up at me. 'Forgive me, Shae. I'm so sorry.'

I looked at Mum, but she had turned away. Her shoulders shook.

'I had an affair,' Dad said. 'It was just the one night. You mother and I had been through so much trying to start our own family. We weren't there for each other.'

'He told me straight away,' said Mum. 'And I forgave him. I blamed myself for pushing him away.'

'I never knew Karen was pregnant until the day you were born. She rang me from the hospital and told me. I went to see you both,' Dad explained.

Mum continued the story. 'I went with your dad even though I didn't want to. I watched him look at you for the first time and I knew I'd never be able to give him that joy, that pure adoration. I didn't want to see you, but my eyes deceived me and I looked anyway.' Her voice broke. 'And I was in love. You were perfect.'

'Karen told me she was giving you up for adoption. I had to agree to it or take you myself,' said Dad.

Aunty Liz was right. I had half-truths. I knew there was an affair and I knew there was a daughter involved. Just the wrong one.

'So, Stella's not your daughter?' Poor Stella. She was going to be crushed.

Dad shook his head. 'I wish she were, if it would save you some of this hurt.'

Everyone watched me. Waiting for my reaction. My mind was on replay. *Karen. Mum. Dad. Stella. Karen. Mum. Dad. Stella.* I swallowed the bile rising inside my throat, clenched my fists and did the only thing I could think of. I fled the room.

Chapter 38

I crossed the highway and turned off the footpath toward the walking track. My legs pumped the pedals up and down. The burning sensation in my lungs threatened to implode, but I pushed on harder, faster. I just wanted to get as far away from the house as I could. Away from the truth I had been looking for all summer holidays. Away from the answers I had been seeking for weeks.

'You're not mine!'

They had been lying to me my entire life. My beliefs, my moral compass, my sense of right and wrong, all came from my parents. Yet it turned out they were the biggest liars of all. How could they keep this from me? Would I have ever found out if Stella hadn't gotten her story wrong? Stella thought her search was over, but really it had just begun. I thought of the woman in the picture, Karen. My biological mother.

I slammed on the brakes and vomited over the path. I choked and coughed and spluttered on their deceit. It was all too much. I couldn't take any more. Mum, Dad, Karen, they were all involved. Even my aunty and uncle knew! For over seventeen years they have all known the truth. That I was the product of a one-night stand, not a loving relationship like I always believed. I gagged as my stomach emptied. This was not happening. It couldn't be real! Stella was older than me, so why did Karen keep her and not me? Was she ashamed by the affair? Did she always plan to give me away or did she decide at the last moment?

I spat out the last of the vomit and wiped my mouth with my sleeve. Back on my bike I kept riding, faster and faster until my calves ached. I pushed through the pain because I couldn't slow down. If I did, the past might just catch up with me. Again.

I kept going until I found myself near the Weir. I stood the bike near a tree and walked down the thin trail. It passed the cave where Mikayla and Brendan pashed that day. I continued past where Simon and I skimmed stones, until I came to the concrete crossing. It seemed so long ago that Lexi played that stupid prank on me. There was no waterfall today even with the rain we had camping. Not even a ripple moved along the surface. I looked across at the great concrete divide and moved out toward it. There was no fear this time, no hesitation, just movement. Once I reached the middle I looked out across the views. I sat down on the narrow ledge and pulled my legs up beneath my chin.

Is this how my life would be now? The two dividing moments that determined my existence. Before I knew I was an unwanted product of a one-night stand, then after I discovered the truth. Stella was right about one thing. She was my sister, but only because we had the same mother. There was no spark of resemblance toward Karen in the photo. If she really was my biological mother, shouldn't I feel some connection to her? My stomach flip-flopped and threatened to explode again.

'Shae!' Lexi made her way toward me. Her forehead was sweaty and her hair was wild. Thankfully, she was alone.

'Can I sit with you?' she asked.

I nodded and crossed my legs. Lexi wasn't even wearing her trademark sunglasses so she must have left the house in a rush. She sat opposite me; her face was etched with concern. We stayed sitting on the ledge, both looking out to the horizon.

'Did you know?' I asked.

She shook her head. 'I promise I didn't. I had no idea your mum wasn't really your mum.'

'My *mum*? Humph, which mother?'

'I'm so sorry, Shae,' she said.

'Remember when you talked about how straight my parents were? How the secret couldn't be that bad?' A lone tear dripped from my chin.

'It's definitely not the secret we were expecting.'

'I wish it was just a stupid affair he was having.' My voice wavered. 'At least nothing else would have changed.'

'Hey, you'll get through this, Shae.'

My chest ached at the knowledge I had gained. My mind burst with new questions.

Lexi gripped my hands tight. 'Shae, you are still the same person we all love. With the same parents who love you.'

'Yeah, except my mother *isn't* my mother.'

'Maybe not biologically, but in every other way she is,' said Lexi.

'Why are you defending her?' I pulled my hands away. 'You're meant to be on my side.'

'I am on your side, I promise.'

'No, you're not. Did they send you after me?' I demanded.

'No!'

'Then why don't you get it? They've lied to me for seventeen years. All this time they could have told me. But. They. Didn't.' The enormity of the secret weighed down on me. No sooner did I have answers when more questions arose.

'I know it's a huge shock, Shayzie. The best kept secret ever and that's saying something in our family. I can't believe even I didn't know about it.'

'Don't make jokes. And don't make this about you, Lexi. You always do that! Not everything is about you.' I turned away from her.

'I'm sorry, I keep saying the wrong things. I understand this is serious, but I'm sure they were just trying to protect you.'

'Don't you dare.' I backed away from her. 'Don't you dare defend them to me. You're meant to defend me. Be outraged, with me!'

Lexi, who had always been like a sister to me, wasn't on my side. The most important thing to happen in my life and she couldn't even support me.

'Just when I need you the most, Lexi, you can't be there for me. Just leave me alone,' I said.

I didn't need her pity filled eyes and pretend concern. All this time I had been confiding in her and for what? So she could defend them and take their side in this unforgivable situation.

'Shae, wait.' Lexi reached for me.

I spun away from her, but my ankle twisted and my foot slipped over the edge. I screamed as I lost my balance.

'*Shae!*' Lexi reached for me.

My arms flailed as I floated through the air and plummeted toward the Weir. The water's surface came up to meet me. Cold water walloped against my back. My neck jolted and a sharp pain rippled through my spine. I tried to call out, but my voice was smothered with water, making a gurgled sound. The Weir water was putrid and muddy. I choked on the foul taste.

I fought the sinking feeling and kicked my legs as the current dragged me along. Just as I was about to get my head above the water, a boulder got in my way. *Thwack!* Darkness spread as I slipped beneath the water.

Chapter 39

My eyes were heavy as I tried to open them. They fluttered, then closed. I sensed movement to the right, then there was pressure on my hand. Muffled sounds surrounded me, like being underwater. A sharp voice called my name.

'Shae? Can you hear me?'

I turned toward the voice as a face blurred into focus. 'Mum?'

She lifted my hand to her mouth. Her kiss was light. My eyes closed and I forced them open again.

'Hey there, you're safe now.' It was Dad's face this time.

The back of my head throbbed. I tried to reach up, but something stopped me.

'Don't touch the bandage,' said Dad, moving my hand away. 'You have stitches.'

That explained the headache, but my entire body was sore. I tried to adjust myself and my limbs screamed in protest.

'What happened?' I asked.

A nurse moved past Dad and checked my blood pressure. It only took a moment before the Velcro was ripped and the band released.

'How's the pain?' she asked.

'Head hurts.'

'I'll speak to the doctor. He might want to see you before he gives you more pain relief.'

I tried to lick my lips, but my mouth was dry. 'Thirsty.'

The nurse passed me a cup of water then left the room. I drank until the cup was empty. Mum sat it on the small table next to the jug. She caressed my cheek and smiled. Her hair was messy and she wore no make-up. Both an unusual occurrence for her.

A machine to the side monitored something. Different lines, for different reasons. A tube was connected to a vein in my hand.

'You're going to be fine, sweetheart,' Mum said.

'What happened to me?'

'What's the last thing you remember?' asked Dad.

I frowned. My mind wandered back, trying to locate the last memory. Magnetic Island with Callen. Snorkelling. My parent's car in the driveway. Lexi's kitchen. Mum and Dad. Stella. Karen. An affair.

I looked at Mum. 'I'm not your daughter!'

'Yes, you are. Don't say that.' She gripped my hand. 'I may not have given birth to you, Shae, but you *are* my daughter. You will *always* be my proudest accomplishment.'

'We love you, Shae. We love you so much. We couldn't bear it if you hated us,' said Dad as he knelt against the bed. 'Shae, we are so sorry. We made a choice and it was the wrong one. We only wanted what was best for you, but you should have known all along. We should have told you from the beginning.'

Mum placed her hand on his head. 'We are sorrier than you could ever know, Shae. You have to forgive us. You just have to!'

I held my hand up. '*Stop!* I don't want to hear any more apologies.' I looked at both my parents, waiting for me to give them something I couldn't. Forgiveness.

'Why am I in hospital?' I asked.

Dad cleared his throat. 'You fell off the Weir.'

'Thank goodness Lexi was with you,' said Mum.

'I was on the Weir?' I couldn't remember anything after the yelling match in Lexi's kitchen. It was just blank in my mind after that.

'Lexi said you slipped and cracked your head on the way down,' Mum explained. 'She pulled you out and got some help. They called an ambulance and we met you here.'

'Where's Lexi now?' I asked.

'Probably still in the visitor room. She's with her friend Callen,' said Dad.

'Can I see them?'

'I'm not sure that's a good idea,' said Dad.

'Because you two have such great ideas?'

'Shae, that's not fair,' said Mum.

'What's not fair is finding out you're not my mother!' It was mean and hurtful but I couldn't help myself.

Her face crumpled 'You're upset. I understand.'

'Maybe you could see them, just for a minute,' said Dad. He pulled Mum away from the bed and they left me alone.

Within seconds Lexi rushed into the room and hugged me. 'I'm sorry, Shae. I shouldn't have argued with you. I'm always on your side, no matter what.'

'Lexi, you saved me.'

'I was really scared when you fell. Then when I pulled you out, I panicked. There was so much blood.' Her face was pale and her eye wide.

'I'm fine, because of you. And for the record, I'm never going on the Weir again.'

'I'm just glad you're going to be okay.' Lexi held me tight.

I looked beyond Lexi and saw my other visitor waiting.

'He's been here the whole time,' she whispered.

Callen stood in the doorway. He flicked the hair from his eye and shoved his hands into his pockets. Lexi blew me a kiss and left us alone.

Callen moved toward the bed. 'Hi, Princess.'

I swatted him feebly, but he grabbed my hand and held tight. He leaned down and rubbed his stubbled skin across the back of it.

'Did Lexi tell you?' I asked.

He nodded.

'I'm so mad at them,' I said.

'It will take a bit of time to get used to, but if anyone can do that, it's you.' He kissed my forehead. 'You parents said only a couple of minutes so I should go. Don't hate them too much. Somebody very wise once told me that sometimes you have to make a choice. Hang on to your anger. Or let it go. It can't be both.'

***

Later that day Mum sat on the edge of the chair and Dad leant against it. Both of them united. 'Shae,' said Dad. 'We understand that we've hurt you.'

'You don't understand anything!' Now that I'd had time to think about things, I realised they still hadn't told me everything.

'You need time and we get that,' said Mum.

'I don't need time, I need answers.'

'Of course. You can ask anything. No more lies,' she said.

'Why was your lawyer following me?'

They shared a look before dad answered the question. 'He was keeping an eye on things in Townsville while we were in Airlie Beach.'

I nearly confessed to knowing about the emails and text messages. Instead, I confessed to something else. 'I went home one day, back to Airlie Beach. I knew something was going on and I wanted to find out what. Instead, I found …' I lowered my voice. 'Money. Heaps of money in the safe.'

Just then the nurse returned with a syringe. 'The doctor said I could give you something a bit stronger for the pain now you've regained consciousness.' She added it into the IV. 'It will make you sleepy, but that's good. You need to rest.'

'No, not yet,' I protested.

'Shae, don't worry. I promise we can explain it, but later okay,' said Dad.

My eyes closed once again.

Chapter 40

The next day Lexi plumped my pillow up. 'Do you need anything else?'

'No thanks, Nurse Allery, that will be all,' I said.

She flopped on the seat as my phone beeped through a text message. Lexi sprung up and passed it to me.

'I hope you're going to be this helpful when I get out of here.'

Thanks for introducing me to your cousin. Hope you feel better soon.

I looked at Lexi questioningly.

'What?'

I shot a text message back to Oliver.

Be nice to her or I will release the frogs!

Oliver was terrified of frogs. When he was a kid, he went to sit on a public toilet seat and three green frogs hopped out from beneath the rim. He ran screaming and has had a crazy phobia ever since.

'So … it was great *Oliver* made it to the party,' I said.

Lexi broke eye contact with me.

'Did you get to talk to him for long?' I asked.

She brushed at her skirt. 'We talked for a while.'

'Liar! You've been holding out on me.'

She scrunched her nose up. 'Maybe a little bit.'

'Lexi!'

I showed her the text message. She squealed and flicked her hair over her shoulder.

'Tell me everything,' I demanded. 'Hang on, what about Kai?' Oliver didn't need him turning up on his doorstep.

'Kai is finished. We're over. I told him the night of the party, just after Blake kicked him out.'

'Can't say I'm sad Kai's gone,' I said.

Lexi sighed. 'I thought about what you said and you were right.'

'I was? About what?'

'About not owing Kai my loyalty. I mean sure he could be sweet at times, but most of the time everything had to be his way. I realised that when I was with him, I thought I could be myself but really, I was changing to suit him.'

I took in everything Lexi said and realised the old Lexi was back. 'So, how does Oliver fit in with all this?'

'Shae he is sooo sweet! We talked at the party and he made me laugh and it was, I don't know, easy. I could just be myself.'

'So, now what?'

'He rang me while you were *frolicking* at the island.' Lexi gave me a knowing look. 'Anyway, we were supposed to meet up that night but then …'

We both knew what happened next.

'But it didn't matter because I met him around the corner from the hospital yesterday. I bought him a milkshake to make up for ditching him. He couldn't believe you were in here.'

'Did you tell him everything?' I asked.

She shook her head. 'I told him your parents weren't splitting up. But I said there was some other stuff going on and you would fill him in when you're ready.'

'Thanks, Lexi.'

The idea of telling my friends I had a sister plus another mother was too weird. I needed a bit more time before it was announced publicly. There was a knock at the hospital door before it opened.

'Stella!' I said, surprised.

She hesitated before entering. 'I hope you don't mind me coming.'

'How did you know I was here?' I asked.

'Callen told me, but I can go if you want?' she said.

'No, come in.' I urged. 'There's someone you should meet.'

Stella moved tentatively closer.

'This is Lexi, my cousin. I guess maybe she's *our* cousin? Lexi, this is my sister, Stella.'

'Are you serious?' said Lexi.

I nodded. 'Yep, it's official. Now you've got two cousins.'

She looked Stella over from top to bottom. 'You've got the same hair,' said Lexi. 'Not the colour, but the fabulous frizz factor.'

Stella and I looked closely at each other. Lexi was right. Stella's hair was light brown but longer than mine.

Stella patted it down. 'I usually straighten it, but I ran out of time today.'

'I feel like I should hug you or something,' said Lexi. 'Would that be weird?'

Stella shook her head. 'I was thinking the same thing.'

'Hey, don't forget the patient.' They moved across to the bed and we managed a group hug of sorts.

'Hey, Stella, there's something you need to know,' I said.

She waved her hand. 'It's fine. I already know.'

'How?'

'Don't be mad at him, but Callen told me about you and my mum.'

'Are you okay with that?' I asked. It was a lot to take in. Trust me, I knew.

'Sure! I still get a sister out of it and that's a bonus.' She smiled, but I could tell she was just trying to be brave.

I reached for her hand. 'You get a sister and four cool cousins. That's a pretty good deal.'

The door opened and three things happened at once. Stella recognised my dad. My parents made the connection with Stella, and Lexi promptly excused herself.

'Stella?' said Dad.

Mum cleared her throat as she took in my half sibling. 'It's very nice that you came to visit Shae,' she managed.

'I can go. I wasn't going to stay long anyway,' she said.

'Don't go.' Mum gestured for Stella to sit down. 'Please, stay a bit longer.'

Stella hesitated before sitting on the edge of the chair. 'I should apologise to you both.'

'Apologise? You've got nothing to be sorry about,' said Dad.

'But I started this whole thing,' she said, miserably. 'If I hadn't poked around then none of this would have happened.'

Mum shook her head. 'It's something we should have dealt with a long time ago. It's not your fault. We're the ones to blame, not you.'

'Stella, I want you in my life.' I turned to my parents. 'She's going to be in my life, no matter what.'

'Shae, she's going to be in *our* lives,' said Dad.

It was strange to watch my parents and Stella talking. They asked her the normal questions. What did she do on weekends? Did she work? Nothing too serious. I hadn't even known she existed and now here she was chatting like she had always been in my life. It was weird but it felt right. Stella laughed at whatever Dad said, and I saw something in her eyes. I knew it from my own reflection. Hope.

My mind wandered to the missing person in all this. The one link that had been uncoupled from the chain. That's when I recognized something else on Stella's face. Something that had been gnawing away inside me. An emotion I had been trying to squash ever since I

221

first looked at that grainy image in the post. *Fear.* Where did Karen fit into all this? My eyes met Stella's. I could have sworn we were just thinking the same thing.

Chapter 41

The first day back at my cousin's house and my parents hovered as if I were a newborn baby. I hoped they didn't act like this for too long.

Mum pouted. 'I know you're fine, but it's my job to fuss and worry about you so just let me do it.'

I sighed. 'Will you at least let me feed myself?'

'I'm not that bad,' she grumbled.

Dad gripped Mum's shoulders. 'Actually, you are.' He sat on the recliner chair next to me while Mum settled on the other one.

'All jokes aside, Shae, you have to let us know if you start getting headaches or feel dizzy,' said Dad. 'Concussion is serious so remember all the things the doctor told you.'

'I will, but I feel fine. My head's a bit sore from the stitches, but that's it.'

'We're taking you home tomorrow. The doctor said you can get your stitches out there,' said Mum.

'Tomorrow? But I can't leave yet.'

'Shae, we want you to come home so we can look after you,' she said.

'It's a bump to the head, no big deal.' I tried not to panic. I wasn't ready to go home to Airlie Beach. There was still some unfinished business here.

'You could have died at the Weir the other day.'

'But I didn't,' I argued.

'There's no compromising here, Shae. Why do you want to stay longer anyway?' asked Mum. 'Is it that boy Callen?'

She had caught us kissing earlier, but he wasn't the reason I wanted to stay longer. Well, not the only reason.

I paused before deciding to tell them the truth. Although I wasn't sure how they would react. I didn't want to hurt my parents, but this was something I had to do. 'Actually, it's Stella. She's asking Karen to meet with me, face to face.'

Dad shook his head. 'No, absolutely not.'

'It's not up to you.' How dare he try and take this away from me? I wanted to meet the woman who gave me up. I wanted to know why she made that decision. I had to meet her to move forward. 'I just want to meet her. I'm not about to start calling her mummy or anything.'

'Shae, I'm not sure it's a good idea,' said Dad.

'It's just something I need to do. And I'm doing it with or without your support. There's no compromising here,' I mimicked Mum.

Neither argued further. Looks like I won that round. 'Now, is this a good time for those other questions?' I asked.

Dad nodded. 'No more secrets, Shae, we promised. What else do you want to know?'

My hands trembled as I pushed my hair behind my ear. Nothing they told me now could be worse than that day in the kitchen. *'You're not mine!'*

'Why did you cancel the trip *and* send me away? Why couldn't I have just stayed at home?'

'Karen had made contact with your mother and I. We were worried about what she might do. Don't forget I only knew this woman for one night. I'm ashamed by this fact, Shae, but it's the truth and I can't change that. Then nine months later I got a call to come and collect our daughter, or agree to give her up for adoption. I didn't have time to process it. I had to decide there and then. Fortunately, your mother … ' he smiled at her, 'agreed with my choice.'

'Do you know what your name means, Shae?' Mum asked.

I shook my head.

'It means a gift. Don't you see Shae? You're our gift.'

Dad continued. 'I didn't know anything else about Karen and she's never made contact all this time. So, when I spoke to her for the first time in seventeen years, I didn't know what she was capable of. I had no idea what game she was playing at, or worse, she might have been psychotic for all I knew. The more insistent she became for us to tell you about her, the more I worried. I had to get you out of the way until I could work out why she'd made contact after all these years.'

'Why did Karen want you to tell me?' I asked. 'Stella thinks it's her fault.'

'Stella certainly sped things up,' agreed Dad. 'But Karen had already contacted me.'

'I don't understand why she contacted you in the first place,' I said.

'You'll have to ask her that.'

'Was she blackmailing you?'

Dad frowned. 'No, why?'

'There was a lot of money in the safe so I wondered … '

Mum and Dad looked at each and laughed.

'What's so funny?'

'You've been watching too many movies, but we did say no more secrets,' said Mum.

'Yeah, except a surprise is different from a secret,' said Dad. 'Some of the money is for your aunty and uncle to visit Aileen. They were too proud to take more than the flight money and we wanted to give them a bit extra.'

'But there was more than enough for flights, unless you're paying for everyone to go,' I said.

Dad didn't say anything.

'You're not, are you?'

'Not quite. The rest of the money is to buy your car. I was waiting for the delivery to pay the balance. Got a better deal for cash! But it was supposed to be a surprise for your 18th birthday.'

'Surprise,' said Mum.

'Oh.' I felt stupid with the other conspiracy theories. Mum leaving Dad, Dad leaving Mum, Karen blackmailing them, Stella blackmailing them. All along it had nothing to do with any of that.

'So, what kind of car is it?'

Dad laughed. 'Oh no, at least that part will remain a surprise.'

They seemed to be happy answering my questions. Finally, they were telling the truth. I decided to keep going. 'What about John, your lawyer? What was he really up to?'

'John was looking into all kinds of possibilities,' said Dad. 'We wanted to be sure the rules hadn't changed and Karen had no legal claim to you.'

'I'll be 18 soon. I'm virtually an adult.'

'Yes, but I adopted you all those years ago,' explained Mum. 'It was more for peace of mind I suppose. Plus, like your dad said, we didn't know why she had made contact after all this time.'

'You know the reason now, don't you?'

Mum sighed. 'We can't tell you.'

'But you said no more secrets!'

'This isn't a secret, Shae. It's just not our story to tell you.'

'Fine, but keep telling me about John,' I said.

'I had John looking into family law, and your dad had him looking into Karen's background, previous law suits, anything that we might need to know. Luckily, she had no ulterior motive and we needn't have gone to all that trouble,' said Mum.

'Well, why did she contact you in the first place then?' I begged. What new secret was being kept from me?

'We're not answering that, Shae. But, if you do meet Karen because that's what you really want, then you can ask her yourself,' said Dad.

I wanted to ask her, but I had another question that meant more. *Why did she keep Stella and not me?*

Chapter 42

That afternoon I dozed on the lounge chair next to the pool. After all their fussing my parents finally agreed I would be able to look after myself while they went to the shops. I didn't bother to put my bikini on. Just being outside in clothes made me feel better. I had been cooped up inside for too long and needed to feel sunshine on my pasty skin.

We would be going back to Airlie Beach soon, but I wasn't ready to go home just yet. This was going to be my last year of high school and it would be a huge year. But I couldn't even think about that, or beyond that for the moment. I had just uncovered a secret mother and sister. Two people that could have been in my life all along but weren't.

The sliding door whooshed open and Simon walked through.

'Do I know you? I got a knock to the head so my memory's a bit fuzzy,' I joked.

Simon's dimpled chin showed through when he smiled. 'How are you feeling?'

'I'd be fine if Mum and Dad stopped fussing.'

'Sorry I didn't come into the hospital,' he said. 'But I wasn't sure you wanted to see me.'

I sat up to look at Simon properly. 'Why wouldn't I want to see you? We're friends, or did you change your mind about that?'

'I didn't change my mind, but I still wasn't sure you'd want to see me after the party ... ' His voice trailed off. 'Anyway, I hoped you would and bought you a 'feel better' present.'

He presented me with a small, round gift from his pocket. I pulled the bow off and tore open the pink paper. 'A shiny rock! You shouldn't have.'

'Thought you could work on your skimming skills,' he teased.

'Thanks, I love it.' I pretended to skim it in Simon's direction.

Simon stood up. 'I have to go, but I'll see you soon, okay.'

I held the rock up to the light and thought about all that had happened this summer. It was so long ago I was disappointed about a cancelled New Zealand holiday. Who knew the holidays would unfold like they had.

'Are you okay out here? Do you need anything?' Lexi interrupted my thoughts.

'Did my parents tell you to check up on me?'

Lexi slipped her sunglasses down. 'Your dad slipped me twenty bucks to keep an eye on you so long as I didn't blab.'

I laughed. 'That sounds about right.'

'Does it hurt?' Lexi moved closer for a look at my damaged head. 'The stitches aren't too bad. They make you look tough.'

'You're such a liar.' I reached for the wound and cringed as I touched the bald place they had to shave to stich up the gash.

She adjusted my hair. 'There, you can't even tell.'

For once I was grateful for my frizzy hair. I pulled on a length that sprung back into place as soon as I let go.

'Stella called,' I said. 'She's waiting for the right moment to ask Karen about meeting me, whatever that means.'

'Is that what you want to do? Meet her?' Lexi asked.

I nodded. Karen must know by now that I know about her. *Was she relieved the secret was out? Did she want to meet me?*

'Well, I think she'd be crazy to pass up the chance to meet you.' Lexi leaned down and hugged me. 'You seem fine out here so I'm just going to take your dad's money and run. Plus, Olly's calling soon.' She skipped inside and left me alone.

A deep voice floated over the fence.

'Of old and new
I want to do
The best by you
I love you true.'

Mr. Sampson sang the next verse.

'Love is a knife
Through all the strife,
You are my life
Please be my wife.'

I climbed the fence carefully and poked my head over. 'Hello, Mr. Sampson.'

'Shae! You look like a sun goddess bursting over the fence like that.'

'Now I know where Callen gets his smooth talking from,' I teased.

'Helps keep me young. My Sally always told me I was a terrible flirt, but she didn't have to worry. I only ever had eyes for her. She was the most beautiful creature God put on this earth, right up until the day she died.'

'You must miss her,' I said.

'I do. That's why I sing to her. But I know we'll be together again one day. Soon enough it will be my turn and she'll be waiting. Do you believe in something, Shae?'

I shrugged. 'We don't go to church or anything like that.'

'I'm not talking about church or religion,' he said. 'I'm talking about believing in something that you know to your core is right. You can't explain it, but nothing anybody said could change your mind about it.'

Once I would have said my parents. Maybe I will again one day.

230

'I'm not sure,' I answered, truthfully.

'I knew Sally was the woman for me, even when she didn't think so. You see Sally didn't want to marry me at first.'

'Really? Why not?'

'Sally couldn't have children. She said it wasn't right I should miss out on something like that. But I knew without a doubt she was the one for me.' Mr. Sampson grinned. 'I wouldn't take no for an answer. It took a long time, but eventually she agreed.'

I thought of Callen's parents. 'Was she wrong about having children?'

'Yes and no.' Mr. Sampson scratched his chin. 'She was wrong because we *were* supposed to spend our lives together. But she wasn't wrong about carrying her own child. We adopted Callen's father, and I thank God every day for that. I say a little prayer every night of gratitude. Knowing his birth mother couldn't give that little boy the life he deserved, meant we got to.'

A lump formed in my throat that wouldn't go away. 'Sally sounds like a special lady.'

'She sure was. Now you take it easy, Shae, especially after your little accident.'

'Thanks, Mr. Sampson.' I started to climb back down the fence.

'And, Shae, thanks for helping my Callen to smile again.' Mr. Sampson walked back toward the house whistling his song for Sally.

Chapter 43

The next day Callen loaded his car with a suitcase and backpack. I hid behind the glass inside Lexi's kitchen watching.

'Aren't you going to say goodbye?' Lexi pushed the curtain aside.

I leant against the kitchen bench. 'Of course, I will, it's just, I don't know what kind of goodbye it is.'

'Shae, go and talk with him. Stop avoiding … whatever this is.'

I grabbed an apple and walked toward the front door. Lexi was right. Callen and I needed to talk. With a deep breath I pushed open the wire door. It slammed behind me and Callen looked up instantly. I put on a bright face, waved and walked toward him.

'Are you all packed?'

He nodded. 'What about you?'

I shrugged. 'I managed to get another day out of my parents. There's one more thing I need to do before I go.'

He leaned against his car. 'So, you're going through with it? You're meeting Karen?'

'Hopefully. Stella's still working on it, but I didn't want to leave before I knew for sure. Either way I need to know where I fit in.'

'Does that include with me?' Callen asked.

I pulled on my necklace. 'Is that what you want?'

Callen looked at the ground and my heart sank. 'Shae I've never—'

'It's fine. You don't need to say anything.'

'Shae, meeting you this summer was the best thing that's happened to me. I was going to say, *I've never* felt like this about someone before.'

'So, you nearly running into me was a good thing?' I asked.

'No, *you* nearly running into *me* was a great thing.' He held my hands. 'Look, I still have things I need to figure out.'

'Callen, I don't want to hold you back from anything.'

'Are you kidding? It's because of you I actually want to do something.' He ran a hand through his hair. 'I spoke to my parents last night and told them everything. The whole Kai story.'

'Woah, that's huge.' I wait to see if he adds more, but he doesn't so I push a bit further. 'What did your parents say about it?'

He doesn't respond immediately, as if choosing his words before speaking. Maybe I shouldn't have pushed. Maybe they were in an even worse place now than before he came to his pop's house.

His hair flopped forward as his head dropped. 'I couldn't believe it, Shae, they apologised. I've never seen dad like that, not even when Gran died. He kept saying how ashamed he was for not being on my side from the start.' He shook his head. 'It was intense, but in a good way in the end.'

My heart soared for him. 'I'm really happy for you.'

'You don't understand, Shae. It's because of *you* I did that. It's because of the courage you've shown that I even had the guts to talk to them. I even rang Fish afterwards. Thought I'd do the whole damn lot!'

'How'd that go?'

Callen nodded. 'I reckon I was even more nervous ringing Fish than telling my parents but ... ' he shrugged. 'It was weird at first and then he started telling me about his little brother and some annoying thing he'd done that day and it was like no time had passed. Like we had just talked the day before. Anyway, we're meeting up tomorrow at the Strand. Gonna just hang out for a bit.'

'You did it. You made a choice.' I grinned.

Callen nodded. 'It couldn't be both, so I chose to let go. Thanks to you.'

Callen lifted my chin up toward him and kissed me. A light kiss that held promise and left me wanting more.

'That's to say thank you. You gave me your trust by believing in me and I don't want to lose it.' He leaned down, kissed my forehead, then got in the car.

I waved after him as he reversed. '*Stop!*'

His car skidded and he looked at me alarmed. 'What's wrong?'

'Don't go, I've got something for you.'

'Don't run,' he called after me.

I fossicked through the mess on my bed and grabbed the present I asked Lexi to get from the shops. I stumbled out the front door, excited to give Callen his present.

'What are you up to?' he said, suspiciously.

I leaned in the window and sat a tiara on top of his head. 'Just a little something to remember me by.'

We kissed again, soft and gentle.

'Thanks, *Princess*,' he whispered.

I moved out of his way and laughed as Callen reversed down the driveway with the tiara still in position. He honked and drove off.

The night sky started to darken as I sat down on the step. The moon was already high. I kept watching as the stars began to twinkle. My ringtone broke into the stargazing. Stella's name appeared on the screen. This was it, the moment of truth. I took a deep breath and answered the call.

'Karen's agreed to meet you, Shae.'

'Really? When?'

'Tomorrow. Does that work?' she asked.

My heart thumped as Stella's words sank in. This meeting was already seventeen years in the making, another night wouldn't kill me. Then I would get to meet my biological mother.

'Where can we meet?'

'I'll text through our address,' said Stella. 'And, Shae, she didn't take much convincing. I wanted you to know that.'

I swallowed the lump that had formed in my throat. 'Thanks, Stella.'

The call disconnected and I went inside.

Lexi hovered at the end of the hallway. 'How did it go? What did Callen say?'

'He kissed me goodbye,' I answered.

'Goodbye forever or goodbye for now?'

'Goodbye for now.'

'Come on,' she said. 'I know exactly what we need.'

Lexi led me toward the kitchen. She pulled out the blender, ice-cream, chocolate topping, ice, milk and the most important ingredient, strawberries. I sat myself at the table and watched her mix our thick shakes. The pieces smooshed together to create something new. It reminded me of my new family situation, a little bit of everything.

Lexi poured a huge glass. 'Of course! Why didn't I think of that sooner?'

'Think of what?' I asked.

'Callen and I can carpool to Airlie Beach. He can visit you and I get to see Olly.'

'That's the silver lining in all of this?'

Lexi laughed. 'Duh, of course.'

'How are things with Olly?' I asked, cautious. I loved my cousin, but Oliver was also a good friend. I wouldn't want to see either of them hurt.

Lexi grinned. 'I told him I want us to hang out as friends and just see where things go and he agreed. So, we're going slow.'

'Friends and slow, that's great. I'm happy for you, Lexi.' And I meant it.

Lexi slurped down her thick shake. 'Mmm, that's so good!'

'Hey, there's something else.' I took a mouthful and shivered as my taste buds exploded. It was good! 'Stella rang and Karen has agreed to meet me.'

'*What?*'

I spun around at my mother's voice. Dad placed a hand on her shoulder, soothing and supportive.

'You knew this was something I wanted to do,' I said. 'It doesn't mean anything more than I want to meet the woman who gave birth to me.'

Mum nodded. 'We understand, Shae, it's just harder to hear than I thought it would be.'

'I love you both, but I'm doing this.'

Dad pulled Mum closer. 'We'll drive you there ourselves. And we'll wait as long as you need us to.'

Chapter 44

The next morning our car pulled up out the front of an old Queenslander house. It was elevated off the ground and the shutters were pulled tight against the windows. The green paint along the trim looked fresh. The matching picket fence enclosed a garden that was lush and green.

Dad looked in the rear-view mirror. 'Are you sure you want to do this?'

I nodded. 'I want to meet her, but I need to do it on my own,' I said.

'We'll be waiting right here. Take as long as you need,' said Mum.

I studied the house that I could have grown up in. The gate squeaked open and I felt my parents watching every step I took. Just as I was about to press the bell, the front door opened. A woman, much older than Mum, stood before me.

'Hello, Shae, I'm Karen.'

Her features were different to the side profile in the picture. I tried to find something similar to my own. I couldn't help feeling disappointed when I didn't. She looked past me toward the car and waved to my parents.

'Do you want to come in? Stella's not home, but we can still talk.'

I stepped over the threshold. There was no turning back now.

The sunlight dimmed as she closed the front door behind us. The hallway travelled deep into the house. Our footsteps echoed on the floorboards, but the rest of the house was silent. Framed photos hung along the hallway, but I didn't look at them. I couldn't face Karen and Stella's memories hung out for all to see.

We stopped at the end in the kitchen. It overlooked a lounge room with plush couches. She directed me to the square kitchen table to sit at.

'Would you like a drink?' Karen asked.

'Yes, please. Some water.'

'Stella wanted to be here, but I thought it would be better if it were just the two of us.'

Karen produced a cold glass of water. Condensation ran down the outside.

'You must have a lot of questions.' Karen sat opposite me.

Her face was weary. Her skin was almost translucent, too pale for someone who lived in Queensland.

'Not really,' I said, harsher than intended. 'It's pretty straight forward. You, my dad, an unwanted pregnancy.'

'Not unwanted,' Karen interrupted. 'Just unplanned.'

I sighed. 'The truth is I didn't want to meet you just to make you feel bad.'

Karen held a squashed tissue in her fingers. She kept changing hands, as though one might squash it smaller than the other.

'I wanted to tell you … ' I faltered before continuing. 'I wanted you to know I've had a good life. My parents have given me everything I could want. Your decision to give me up is okay.'

'Do you think I need your forgiveness?' Karen said. 'Is that why you think this is all coming out now?'

Her tone was calm and the words hit me hard. I was confused. Why else would she make contact now?

'Shae, it wasn't me who started this family tree adventure,' explained Karen.

I couldn't speak.

'Stella began searching. She poked her nose into things that didn't concern her.'

'How could it not concern her? I'm her sister.'

'Biologically yes, but unfortunately Stella was searching for one family member and instead she got another.'

'But she photographed you and my dad together. You must have started it.'

Karen sighed, followed by a wheezing cough. She covered her mouth with a tissue. It was stained with blood when she removed it.

'That's true. I did contact your father. It was the first time since you were born.'

'Why now?' I demanded. 'If you didn't want anything to do with me, why now?'

My legs shook with nerves. Did I really want to know the answer? Karen's breathing was shallow. She gripped the table and a pained expression passed as she adjusted her position.

'I'm sick, Shae.' She tried to muffle the bout of coughing that erupted. 'Actually, I'm dying.'

Another fit of coughing engulfed her as if to prove the point. She covered her mouth and again the tissue came away red.

'Lung cancer,' she said, matter of factly. 'Don't feel bad for me though. It's my own fault. I always meant to give up smoking.'

Her news sank in and I couldn't believe what I was hearing. 'So, you're *dying* and you *still* didn't want to meet me, is that what you're saying?'

'I promised your parents I would stay out of your life,' her voice wavered. 'I nearly broke that promise many times over the years, but I knew it wouldn't be fair to anyone if I did. It sure wouldn't change what happened.'

'But you did break it. You contacted Dad when you could have just died.'

'That was the plan, to just die,' said Karen shaking her head. 'But I thought your dad should know, just in case. If we're being honest then maybe I hoped he would talk me into meeting you, just once. He wouldn't have even had to tell you who I was.'

'So, Dad could know you were sick, but not me?'

'That was the agreement.' She nodded.

'Then Stella intervened,' I said, putting the rest together.

'She believed he was her father. She often asked about her dad. I always told her she was a gift to me from him.'

'Do you know what your name means, Shae?' Mum asked. 'It means a gift.'

Maybe Stella and I weren't that different.

Karen looked out the window. 'Stella's father was a musician, a free spirit. Stella is so much like him. We were in love for three glorious months. Then he went on tour and I never saw him again.'

I understood everything now. 'Stella was searching for her dad and instead she found a sister.'

Our eyes met as Karen pulled on her necklace, just like I was. Suddenly, she started coughing again. It was harsh, not like earlier. It sounded like she was choking. Karen pushed herself up against the table and clutched at her chest. She shuffled toward the couch. I jumped up and supported her arm. She leant against me as I helped her sit down.

'Oxygen,' she panted.

I dragged over the cylinder with a thin, clear tube attached. She adjusted it over her ears and inserted the hose pieces. A quiet hissing released the pure oxygen. Karen's eyes closed and her face relaxed. I watched the rise and fall of her chest as though she had just run a race around the oval. I searched her face again for any similarities between us. Our eyebrows? Our nose? Our jawline? Her eyes fluttered open.

'You need to rest. I should go,' I said.

She grabbed my arm and pulled the mask from her face. 'Will you come back another day?' Her face was hopeful. 'Now I've broken my promise … I would like to see you again.'

Her breath rattled and she pushed her hair from her face. A small mole sat near the base of her ear on her neck. I reached up and ran my finger along the identical one that sat on my neck.

I nodded. 'I would like that.'

'Shae, I lied. I want your forgiveness. I was selfish back then … I didn't think I could raise two kids on my own.' Her voice broke. 'What a mess I made. I hope in time you can forgive me.'

'Maybe it's not my forgiveness you need.' I squeezed her hand. 'Maybe it's your own.'

I knew in that moment Karen didn't want to be my mother, but she did want to have me in her life.

'I'm grateful I had the chance to meet you, Shae.'

I wanted Karen to be a part of my life, even if it was for a short time. 'I'll come back again. We've got lots to catch up on,' I said.

I walked down the hallway slowly, this time taking in the framed photos. Karen and Stella together, Karen on her own. Stella at different ages. I thought of Stella, my surprise sister. I never knew something was missing from my life. Now that I knew, I didn't want to waste a moment. This summer had changed us all in lots of ways. It was going to be weird having these new people as part of my family, but we were all going to be okay. No more secrets.

The End

Acknowledgements

Summer Change is my love letter to Townsville. When I was fourteen, I spent time living with my cousins in far north Queensland at a place called Townsville. It was a difficult time in my teenage life and as a result I loathed being there. I have visited Townsville many times since those tumultuous years. I have come to realise that it was not Townsville I disliked, but the situation that put me there.

Townsville is a beautiful city to visit with a stunning waterfront and many things to do and explore. Upon reflection, there were many fun and joyful moments of my time there. As a result, I have tried to incorporate as many locations as possible in and around Townsville that made me happy. *Summer Change* is a celebration of those good memories.

In loving memory of my cousin Carol Aileen Pitts (1977 – 2003).
You are still the ultimate Gobbledok!

Please note the locations in *Summer Change* are real but the story is fiction, although the frog reference is true, and I'm still scared of frogs!

My sincere gratitude to Rochelle Stephens and all the incredible people at Wombat Books/Rhiza Press/Rhiza Edge for helping to shape and polish *Summer Change* into the story it is. The edits, suggestions and feedback along the way were so supportive and collaborative. This made it extremely satisfying to work within such a wonderful team of creators.

Thank you to the *The Maurice Saxby Writers Mentorship Program* which offered me a once in a lifetime immersion opportunity into the world of writing based on my submission of the original manuscript that was *Summer Change*. During the two weeks of the program I was inspired, motivated, challenged and supported to grow as an author. A special mention to Helen Chamberlin (Order of Australia for services to literature 2023) for chaperoning me throughout the program and Rosalind Price who was the first person to read the whole manuscript and offer such valuable feedback about *Summer Change*.

To my beautiful family who I love with all my heart. Jamie, Toby and Molly, you all indulge me with my ramblings about story ideas and the writing projects I happen to be working on. You encourage me just by listening and giving me time to write.

My reading/writing friends who have read extracts and even the whole manuscript then provided valid and thoughtful feedback, thank you.

And to you, the reader, thank you for your support by being enticed and picking up *Summer Change*. It is a story of change, resilience and finding your way. May your own journey be smooth and satisfying.

Remember to always Dream Big ... Read Often.

Melissa Wray lives on the Bellarine Peninsula with her husband and two children. Most of her adult life she has been based in Australia, aside from a short trip to London. It was then that she developed a love for travel and exploring and visited many incredible places including Egypt, Turkey, Italy, Spain and Africa. Her travel highlights include La Tomatina (tomato throwing festival in Bunol, Spain) and Carnivale` (festival of masks in Venice, Italy).

Melissa is a teacher who is passionate about education, in particular literacy, and believes the ability to read and write gives power to change. Melissa has completed a *Master of Education* with a thesis by research about picture story book use in the classroom. She uses them in her classroom every chance she gets.

Summer Change is Melissa's third YA novel. *The Ruby Locket* was released in 2020 and *Destiny Road* in 2012. Melissa was selected for *The Maurice Saxby Writers Mentorship Program* in 2015. Her work has won honourable mentions and she has featured in several anthologies.

Melissa is a lover of beautiful smelling candles that she burns constantly when writing, and yummy chocolate that she may, or may not, have hidden behind a specific picture frame at any given time. Vague details are required to deter her family from searching for it.

Melissa believes everyone should Dream Big … Read Often